SAINT STERLING

GEORGIA PEACHES, BOOK 2

VANESSA GRAY BARTAL

DRY CREEK PRESS

Be best. It was the motto by which Sterling Thompson had tried to live his entire life. Every day in every way, he had tried to be perfect, to be all things to all the people in his world. Best son, best friend, best boyfriend, best brother, best business owner. Where had it gotten him? His girlfriend cheated on him with his best friend, his sister moved halfway across the world, his business was sinking, and he was once again living with his mother, trying to help order her life while keeping his father afloat. He had a mental breakdown, tried to jump off a building, ended in a psych ward, and was now on medication that would probably accompany him for the rest of his life. Despite his efforts, Sterling was not best. He wasn't even good. His life was currently being held together with fairy wishes and sticky notes.

"Party tonight."

Sterling didn't need to glance up to know who spoke, but he did anyway. His—former?—best friend stood in the entryway of his bedroom. "You've got to be joking." It was only a few months ago that Duncan got Sterling's girlfriend pregnant at a different party.

"Nope," Duncan said, empty of remorse and self-awareness as usual. How and why had they been friends the last twenty-nine years?

It was a mystery that deepened for Sterling more and more. "Guess where it is."

"No."

"Alby's house."

Sterling looked up again. There was a name he hadn't heard in a long, forgotten time. "Why?"

Duncan shrugged. "She wants to reconnect with the old gang, I guess."

"Why?" Sterling repeated, puzzled. He had no desire to connect with the old gang, despite the fact they all lived in the same town. It was why he'd done his best to avoid them the last decade. And now that he'd sunk so far, he wanted to see them even less.

"That's Alby for you," Duncan said. "What time should I pick you up?"

"Hmm, I'm going to go with never."

Duncan huffed. "Sterling, come on. How long are you going to be mad at me?"

"I'm not mad," Sterling lied. "But we're almost thirty. Isn't it time to stop partying?"

"First of all you have to stop using thirty like some kind of magic timeline. It's only a number. Second, it's not that kind of party. It's at Alby's house. Steaks will be involved. When's the last time you had a steak? Plus, this is probably the last hurrah before the baby comes. I'm leaving tomorrow, traveling for business. When I get back, the baby's coming."

That was a good point, especially about the steaks. However, "I really don't know if I can gear myself up for a visit with the old gang."

"We'll make an appearance and get out if it's bad. Come on, throw Alby a bone. You know she needs it." His tone was teasing, sarcastic, the same tone people always used about Alby.

"If we go, you have to be nice to her," Sterling said, jutting a finger at him. People would try their best to be mean to Alby, it seemed to be the way of it. But Sterling had never allowed such a thing on his watch.

Duncan held up his hands in surrender, grinning because he knew he'd won. "When am I ever not nice?"

Sterling rolled his eyes, but too late, Duncan was already gone. Sterling was desperate enough to wish him back again. He stared at his laptop, a sinking feeling in his gut. Ever since his little sister left to take a job on a cruise ship, he'd been doing his own books, and the news was abysmal. If he didn't find a major influx of cash, and quickly, his shop was finished. But where was he supposed to find such a thing in their tiny hometown? Should he take out a loan? The bookstore was all he had, the only proof he was a functioning adult and not a total failure of a human, as he was beginning to suspect. Even Duncan, with all his many faults, was gainfully employed as a salesman, made a pile of money, owned a car and his grandparents' ancestral farmhouse. Sterling lived with his mom and owned the decrepit sedan he'd had for the last eight years. And it hadn't been new to begin with. He was so tired of struggling, grasping for every mouthful, every day of survival. And then there was his depression on top of it. Sterling could never quite figure out if he had a chemical imbalance or if his life was really that bad. Maybe he wasn't depressed for no reason. Maybe he was in the midst of a normal reaction to his mundane, pathetic existence.

Times like these he missed Birdie something fierce. His sister would tell it to him straight, but she would say it with compassion. Speaking the truth in love, their former preacher would call it. It was what Sterling needed occasionally, more often than not lately, a swift kick in the pants from someone wearing soft and fuzzy slippers. A hand shoving him in the back, urging him in the right direction. Ever since Birdie departed for Europe, Sterling felt like a top someone left spinning. He was working hard but he lacked direction, was going nowhere. And the panicky feeling of failure clung to him from sunup until sundown and often in between. More often than not he woke in the middle of the night, sitting up in bed, covered in sweat and panting, a feeling of certain doom overtaking him. His thirtieth birthday loomed like a harbinger of misery. Being in your twenties and being a mess was expected. But being thirty and a mess meant you might actually be a screwup.

He closed his laptop and wandered into Birdie's room, pausing to sit on her bed. He loved his sister, had always adored her. He had never understood people who fought with their siblings. What was the point? To him Birdie had always been a built-in best friend, the only other person in the world who understood what it was like to grow up in their tumultuous household. She'd had his back from the get go, and he'd had hers. And now she was in Europe living her best life with his former enemy. Life was unpredictable sometimes. Sterling was happy for her, wouldn't wish her back for anything. But he was so lonely he felt like he was drowning. Without her, the onus of both their parents was on him. His mother's everyday problems like the water softener and car troubles and his father's own shaky mental wellbeing.

His glance slid to Birdie's desk. A book lay there. Drawn to books like a magnet to metal, he stood and reached for it, smiling as he read the title. *Mend Over Matter.* He never would have guessed that day Birdie bought the book how much it would end up changing her life. He flicked it open and started to read. "Chapter One: The You You Want To Be!" *What's a you you?* He grimaced, reading the schlocky pop-psychology drivel. Why did he stock this nonsense in his store? Still, he kept reading, making his way through the feel good garbage until the book was over. And then he remained on Birdie's bed, staring into space. Who was he? And, a better question, who was he turning into? Like usual lately, he had no answers. But maybe he was finally beginning to ask the right questions.

"What are you doing in here?" Duncan asked. He had let himself in again as usual. It would probably never occur to him to knock, in case he was not wanted. In Duncan's world, he was always beloved. He wandered around Birdie's room, touching things with unconscious melancholy. If Sterling were a different kind of person, he would take pleasure in Duncan's heartache, the first of his life and caused by Birdie, no less. But he didn't. Mad as he still was at him, Duncan's sadness merely compounded his own heartache.

"Thinking about stuff."

"You Thompsons and your thinking things," Duncan said. He plopped onto the bed beside Sterling and flopped backwards, staring up at the ceiling. Sterling lay down beside him. Birdie had taped an oversized picture of Jane Austen on her ceiling, and they both smiled. "You know we had our first kiss in this bed."

"Way, way too much information for a brother to hear," Sterling said.

"It was only a kiss." He sighed. "Nothing is the same without her. I can't believe she chose Paxton over me."

"She didn't. She chose Italy over you. Paxton followed her, remember?"

"Still, how could she choose anything over me? How could we see things so differently? Birdie has always been my destiny. Why doesn't she know it?"

"Why did you wait twenty nine years to tell her?" Sterling asked.

"I thought it was one of those things that didn't need to be spoken, something that was understood," Duncan mused.

"Is anything like that? Everybody needs some words of affirmation now and again." He scowled, almost certain he had read those exact words ten minutes ago in *Mend Over Matter*. What was it with that book? Was it going to be like a handful of brain worms set loose in his head?

"This is all because she thought about things too much," Duncan said ruefully.

"I guess you would see it that way," Sterling returned.

"What way?"

"With yourself as the victim."

"How am I not the victim?" Duncan asked. "I put myself out there, told her I loved her, and she went away."

"You told her you loved her in the midst of getting my girlfriend pregnant," Sterling pointed out.

"Now who's making it about him?"

Sterling put his hands over his face and scrubbed. "Duncan, I swear."

"Now you sound like Birdie," Duncan said fondly.

"Exasperated beyond all measure?" Sterling guessed.

"Yeah. My point is, you gotta stop thinking about stuff. That's what gets your brain in such a whirl. Be more like me."

"No."

"Act first, think later."

"And how's that working out for you, Dad?"

Duncan grimaced. "I'm not a dad yet. I have a few weeks left."

"In my book, you become a dad the moment the egg is fertilized," Sterling said.

"That's why we never read the same books," Duncan said.

"You mean that's why you never read any books," Sterling said.

"Same difference." He sat up. "You ready to go or what?"

"No."

"What else you got to do tonight? Stare at your sister's ceiling and ponder life's more depressing questions."

Sterling paused. Doing the same thing over and over wasn't working. Time for something else. "You make a good point." He heaved himself up and followed Duncan to the car.

CHAPTER 2

Albertine Mowry lived on the edge of town in what could properly be called a mansion, at least compared to every other house in town. In high school it had been their hangout place, the house with an in-ground pool, game room with pool table, foosball, and—when the Mowrys' heads were turned—plenty of alcohol. Sterling and Duncan had been popular, thanks in large part to being nice looking and playing football. Albertine Mowry, Alby to all but the cruelest of kids, had been part of their set for as long as he could remember. But not because she was likewise popular. If she hadn't been rich with a party house, if her parents hadn't employed half the town, she would have been at the bottom of the heap—a mousy little doormat, alone and rejected.

Four years ago, her parents were killed in a plane crash. The town had been devastated, not only for the loss of such fine, upstanding citizens, but because if the Mowrys' company went, the town would go with it. It was, hands down, the town's largest employer. Like everyone in town, Sterling went to the funeral. It was the last time he saw Alby, and the memory wasn't pleasant. She, so tiny and alone, a little zombie in black. Sterling wished someone would come along and support her, but they'd never shared the sort of closeness that would render him that person. She'd been peripheral to his life, hovering at the edge of every group photo the way she hovered at the edge of every memory. He'd known Alby all his life, and yet until Duncan mentioned her, he forgot her completely.

Now he and Duncan stood on her doorstep, waiting to gain entry.

"Man, this old house never gets any less impressive, you know?" Duncan whispered. The matching doors were massive, at least eight feet of solid wood. Sterling didn't have enough time to answer before they were pulled open. Alby stood on the other side, diminutive in a blue sundress, beaming up at them.

"Duncan and Sterling. How're y'all?"

"Hey, Alby," Duncan said. He picked her up under one arm and kissed her cheek. One thing Sterling had always appreciated about Duncan was that he never went for the easy mark, had never in all his memory teased Alby the way some kids in their group did. If it had been anyone else, he would have said Duncan harbored a little soft spot for her, but that description didn't fit with the friend he knew. Duncan's only soft spot was for Duncan. Alby returned his squeeze, kissing his cheek in return. Sterling had never teased her, either. As far as he knew, they were the only two. Duncan set her down and she turned her attention to him.

"Hey, Sterling, it's good to see you."

"You, too, Alby. How's Atlanta been treating you?" After the death of her parents, she moved to Atlanta. Sterling had no idea who ran her company now, but he hadn't heard anything about it going under. In fact, it seemed to have grown and gotten stronger, if the rumors were to be believed.

"Oh, I've been back for ages," she said, tucking her hair behind her ears. He had forgotten how tiny she was. Belatedly, it occurred to him he should hug her, as Duncan had, but if he did it now it would be obvious and awkward. That was one thing he didn't need in his life, to give Alby ideas. As far as he knew, she'd never dated anyone. He thought it wouldn't take much for her to develop a crush on him. Strangely, the thought didn't repulse him the way it once might have. Alby was a cute little thing, not a stunner by any stretch, but nicely put together features above a well-proportioned body. He wondered if she had still never dated anyone and looked away, shaking his head. He was having thoughts. About *Alby. Oh, how the mighty have fallen.*

"How's your shop?" she asked.

"It's goin'," he said, aiming for an easy smile and failing mightily.

"I love it that you have that, that you're finally embracing that inner nerd you tried so hard to hide forever." She reached out and poked him, smiling.

"I don't remember hiding it," he said. He'd always enjoyed learning, always earned good marks, always been a reader.

"You must have forgotten that time *Great Expectations* fell out of your bag and you dove on it like it was a live grenade before any of your team could see," she said.

"No, you've got it all wrong. See, the entire football team was crazy for Dickens, couldn't get enough of the guy. I was protecting it before anybody could swipe it."

She laughed and covered her mouth with her hands, a habit he'd forgotten. It was as if she purposed to make herself as tiny and invisible as possible, and he wondered why.

Duncan's eyes shifted back and forth between them. Alby swiveled and faced the patio. "Come on y'all. We're outside tonight."

Duncan nudged him. *You're flirting with Alby,* he mouthed.

Sterling shook his head furiously. *Being friendly.*

Duncan quirked an eyebrow at him. Sterling elbowed him hard in the gut. Alby opened the sliding glass door and announced them with a flourish. "Duncan and Sterling are here, y'all." Everyone turned to look, raising their glasses with a cheer.

"Our rightful quarterback and team captain has arrived, y'all. Give a holler," Hogue, former teammate and massive hulk of a guy, bellowed on sight of Sterling.

He began to remember why it had been ten years since he'd had anything to do with anyone from school outside of Duncan. It was like being fifteen all over again, and the feeling wasn't one of pleasant nostalgia. Things had been so difficult in high school. His home life had been in chaos. More often than not it was Sterling who felt like the man of the house as his father sank under the weight of mental illness. And when his father had been lucid, it seemed his sole focus was on Sterling and his illustrious career as a high school football player. For two years, sophomore and junior, he'd been the quarterback. Then his rival, Hayden Paxton, attended some fancy training camp, bulked up, and won quarterback senior year, along with a scholarship everyone believed rightfully belonged to Sterling. Sterling, unable to afford one of the more prestigious colleges without a scholarship, instead stayed home and put himself through community college, continuing to stew in his parents' turmoil, seemingly the lone support for both of them. In college his parents got divorced, easing some of the terrible tension. But for Sterling it merely meant his time and attention were now divided between two houses. Still, it was better than when he was a kid and had felt so much weight on his too-young shoulders. No wonder he had disappeared as much as possible to escape the bad memories. For all the contact he'd had with everyone but Duncan, they might have been living on different planets.

Sterling put up a hand and gave a self-conscious wave.

"They're not going to let you get away with just that," a new voice said, coming up to stand on his right. "Ten bucks says you're tossed in the pool within thirty minutes."

"Hey, Bess," Sterling said, his tone tentative. He and Bess had been something of an item for a bit in high school. He wasn't quite certain where they'd left off. He remembered a lot of drama, but it had been ten years.

"Hey, Sterling," she said, bumping his shoulder without giving him a look. "I see you didn't get beat with the ugly stick in the intervening years."

"You're doing mighty fine yourself," he said, bumping her shoulder in return. The girlish bloom was gone, but she was still a beauty. Her hair was shorter now, and that was a shame. He had always liked to see it long and lying prettily on her back. "How's life?"

"A daily kick in the teeth," she said, her eyes meeting his and practically searing them with a raw sort of pain. "How's yours?"

"The same," he agreed and turned his attention to the scene in front of him. Hogue had tapped a keg and was beginning to chug. Sterling let loose a little sigh. The polite thing to do would be to ask Bess why life was hard, but he couldn't. He had no room in his emotions for anyone else's problems. "I guess some things never change," he noted, eyeing Hogue.

"That's so," Bess agreed. "But then some things change very much." She sounded as weary as he felt. Again he wondered why, and again he pushed away from the feeling, refusing to get himself involved.

Alby came up on his other side. It was likely not a mindless act on her part. In high school, Bess had often been cruel to Alby, often made her the target of attacks. Though Sterling doubted Bess would do the same tonight, he shifted slightly, unhappy with his role as intercessor, intentional or not.

"It would appear that everyone is here," she said, so softly he wondered if she was talking to herself. She touched her hand gently to his arm and glanced up at Sterling with a soft smile. "Sterling, would you mind manning the barbecue for me?"

It was an odd request, but Alby had never been anyone's idea of normal, and Sterling found that he was glad to have a task.

"Absolutely," he said, flashing her a smile.

"Thank you. Follow me, please." She set off for the large brick barbecue. Sterling could easily have walked beside her, but then he would have been required to make conversation. Trailing in her wake gave him a destination without the necessity of making small talk, and for that he was thankful. Multiple people attempted to waylay him; Sterling pointed to Alby as an excuse not to stop. At last they landed by the barbecue. Alby lit it and turned to him with a slight flourish. "There are burgers, brats, steaks, and hot dogs."

"Sounds like I'm about to be a genuine short order cook," he said.

She shook her head. "Everything is seasoned and ready to go. All you need to do is control the flames."

"Yes, ma'am," he said, reaching for the spatula and beginning to load the grill.

"Thank you, Sterling," Alby said before disappearing again.

Sterling eyed the steaks as he slid them on the grill. They were huge, a good cut, and must have cost a fortune. Alby had always been generous, buying everyone in their circle a Christmas or birthday gift, handing out Valentine cards, candy, cookies, and homemade treats. At the time it had seemed normal, but now it was odd. What other seventeen-year-old girl gave so many gifts to her friends?

"Aw, man, how'd you get roped into active service?" Hogue said, striding to the grill, Stokes and Reams in his wake.

Sterling turned to them with what he hoped was a congenial smile. "Alby needed help, and I don't mind."

"Alby's always needed help," Hogue said, and Stokes snickered. Sterling didn't reply, turning instead to survey the hundreds of dollars of meat on the grill.

"Alby's okay," Sterling said mildly, and the subject was dropped. It didn't feel right, to make fun of a woman who was feeding them, but then it had never felt right to make fun of Alby. Not that Sterling had never partaken, but things were different now. *He* was different now.

"You bring other clothes?" Reams asked.

Sterling's hand tensed on the spatula. "Why?"

"In case we toss the ball later," Stokes explained.

"Nah," Sterling said. "Didn't think of it."

"Didn't think of it?" Hogue chimed in. "You're our fearless leader."

Sterling frowned slightly, not following his logic. What did being a high school football captain have to do with bringing extra clothes to a party?

"I guess we're going to have to do this the hard way then," Hogue said.

Before Sterling could turn to ask him what he was talking about, Reams and Stokes had already picked him up. He barely had time to lob his phone onto a chair before he was roughly tossed into the pool. When he came up sopping wet, surrounded by laughter, his eyes fell on Bess. She raised her eyebrows and tapped her watch.

He shook off like a dog, wondering what to do. What he wanted most was to go home and forget this night. He had tried to come back, to fit in, and he had failed. Chalk it up to a lesson learned and move on. But to leave now would be to lose face, and Sterling wasn't so mature or so far removed that he could do that. But neither did he want to stand around all night in soaked clothing, shivering wet and trembling like a drowned kitten.

"Sterling," Alby said, sidling up next to him again. "Would you like to borrow something to wear?"

He eyed her. "I don't think we're the same size, Alby." She was tiny, not having grown since early high school days.

"Silly," she said, shaking her head. "Come with me."

He followed her once again, this time back towards the house. Hogue was guffawing, great stupid laughs of someone who was already drunk. Sterling's hand tightened into a fist, wanting to pound him, for all the old reasons and some new ones, too. Alby clasped his hand, and he glanced at her in surprise. She gave his hand a little squeeze and smiled as if she knew what he was thinking. Alby had always inhabited her own world but maybe she saw more than he gave her credit for. Or maybe his simmering rage was so obvious even she could see it. Whatever the reason it worked to calm him, and he squeezed her hand in return, causing a pink blush to steal over her cheeks. She opened the door to the house and didn't touch him again.

He followed her down the hall to a bedroom on the left. Alby rifled a drawer and handed him a hoodie and jogging pants. She turned to go, but he spoke, "Am I stealing your boyfriend's clothes, Alby?"

"Husband," she said, and Sterling froze. Alby was married? Times had changed. Noting his shock, she shook her head. "That was me joking, Sterling. They're my cousin's. He leaves stuff here for when he swims." She glanced at the drawer, her ever-present smile dimming slightly. He wondered why, but of course he didn't ask. He and Alby hadn't actually been friends. Had anyone been friends with Alby? If so, he couldn't think who. Sterling knew her because she had been the equipment manager for both the football and the basketball teams. And of course she had a party house. Otherwise she likely wouldn't have been accepted into their group. As it was, there had only ever been a certain grudging tolerance for her, a weird sort of social obligation because she was rich and always around, more than a desire to actually have her there. In practically every memory he had of high school, Alby was in it, hovering somewhere in the background. And yet he wasn't certain they'd ever had an actual conversation.

"Sterling, can I ask you something," she said, picking at an invisible spot on her shirt.

He tensed, sensing whatever it was could be bad. Was she about to hit on him? He had never observed a crush on Alby's part. Rather, she had always gazed at him in an adoring sort of way, as a little sister might a big brother. "What?" he asked.

"How's your store doing, really?"

He blinked, tensing further, wondering how honest he wanted to be. Which was better, pride or starvation? He shook his head, unable to say the cursed words. "Not well, Alby."

"Would you like a job?" she asked, glancing up at him with her customary shy smile.

"Doing what exactly?" he asked.

"Project manager," she said.

He sank onto the bed, forgetting he was wet and would likely mar the pristine bedspread. "Alby." He let out a breath. "Honey, why are you offering me a job?"

"'Cause you need money and I need a good project manager," she said.

That was true enough, at least on his part. He was nearly desperate for cash. And now he was being offered a hand up, from Alby of all people. "What makes you think I'd be good at it?" he asked. Was this merely more hero worship? Offering the old team captain a plum position as a way to gain further entrée into their circle of friends? Or, worse, was it pity?

"I know you, Sterling. You'd be good at it," she said with quiet confidence.

He blinked at her, eyes burning, throat thick. Her company paid well. It was a dream of most locals to work there, an assurance they'd be able to make it, to provide for their families. Competition was fierce, and now Alby was offering it up on a silver platter. She resumed her smile and turned away. "I'll get you a bag for your wet things." She left the room before Sterling could reply, but he had to say yes, didn't he? He would likely make a generous salary, plus benefits. He'd be a fool to say no. *Wouldn't be the first time,* he thought. Belatedly remembering his wet clothes, he hopped off the bed and stripped.

CHAPTER 3

When Sterling returned to the party, the food was nearly ready. Alby had taken up the slack on his grill duties. Sterling paused at the edge of the vast outdoor space, watching. She flipped the meat onto the plate with precision, an earnest expression on her face. He hadn't thought of Alby one time in the last ten years, not one moment of curiosity over her. But if he had, he would have pictured her this way—working, oblivious to the party atmosphere around her. She had never actually partaken in any sort of merriment, no beer pong, no downing of shots, no making out, no dancing. Had she even laughed? It was hard to remember through his own alcohol-soaked haze, but somehow he thought not. And now, ten years later, it was still the same. Everyone around her was becoming increasingly inebriated, save Sterling, while Alby carefully manned the fire. She was so...*good*, he realized. Alby easily achieved the sort of perfection he'd always aimed for. How odd that people had looked to him as a paragon when Alby had been right there the whole time, leading by example for anyone who took the time to notice. High school being what it was, absolutely no one ever took the time to notice, Sterling included.

He took a fortifying breath and eased closer. "Sorry about that."

"Wasn't your fault," she said easily. Plating the last of the steaks, she turned off the grill. "Food's ready, y'all."

Sterling chuckled at her soft tone. "Oh, Alby," he muttered before putting his fingers to his mouth and emitting a piercing whistle. Everyone came to a standstill and gave him their attention. "Food." He pointed to the overloaded platters.

People began herding toward them. Sterling lost sight of Alby, but then he wasn't actually looking for her. When he caught sight of her later, she was bustling around, serving as always, foisting iced tea and cornbread on people.

"I suppose some things never change," Bess remarked, eyeing Alby. Somehow she had ended up sitting next to him at the wooden outdoor table while Duncan seemed to be having a game of who can get the drunkest and stupidest with Hogue, Reams, and Stokes. "Once a doormat, always a doormat."

Sterling didn't disagree, but neither did he chime in. Back in the day Bess had led the underground campaign to torment Alby, to make sure she understood how thoroughly she would never fit in. Right now he couldn't tell if she was continuing to do so or merely stating fact. Alby was a doormat. She would be one for as long as she continued to let them walk all over her and, judging by the people happily eating her free and delicious food, the gravy train wasn't ending any time soon.

"It's like time stopped," Sterling said. "Do you guys come here often?"

Bess gave him a little frown. "No. I haven't been here since we graduated. What, you think Alby and I spend our weekends together?"

"I don't know. Everything feels a little surreal, like I went away and grew up but everything else stayed the same," Sterling said.

"Everything definitely changed," Bess said. "We all changed, Sterling." The tone was back, the longsuffering one.

"What's up, Bess?" Sterling asked and almost sighed in relief when she shook her head. He'd lost touch with Bess, the same way he'd lost touch with everyone. For two people who lived in a small town, their lives couldn't be farther apart. After high school, he and Duncan started to hang out with their college friends and then, when college was over, only each other.

"Feeling my age, I guess," Bess said. At the end of the table, Reams and Hogue were having a competition to see who could eat the most steak the fastest, Duncan and Stokes cheering them on.

"Think Reams will beat him this time?" Sterling said, for lack of anything better.

"No. Hogue will win," Bess said without looking at either man. "Where'd you get the clothes? Alby have a secret man stash?"

"Apparently," Sterling said, plucking at the hoodie. He remembered Bess's prediction that he would be tossed into the water. "Have you turned psychic?"

"No, but I've lived it all before. Ten years have come and gone and it's still like yesterday, you know?"

"Not really," Sterling said.

"No, I guess not for you. I've been a bit envious of the way you've managed to pull away, gain some distance from all this," Bess said.

"You shouldn't be," Sterling said seriously. He might not still be enmeshed with the high school crowd, but he was a mess in other ways.

"Want to talk about your trauma?" Bess offered.

"No. Want to delve into yours?" Sterling countered.

"Not even a little," Bess said. They shared a smile and finished eating a few bites in silence.

At the end of the table, Hogue hollered, pounding his palm on the table, declaring himself the winner.

"Right again, Bess," Sterling said.

"It wasn't a big leap," Bess said, and Sterling agreed. Hogue was a big guy, tall and burly; he had always been able to pack it away, and he hated to lose anything.

"So, what's going to happen next?" Sterling asked.

She looked at him, considering. "You and I are going to retire to that quiet, cozy corner across the way." She nodded toward the other side of the pool.

Sterling picked up his glass, staring at it as he considered. Did he want to get something started with Bess again? There was always the chance it could lead to something more, something he didn't want. But maybe, like him, she merely wanted to knock the edge off her frayed emotions for the night. He set down the water and stood. "Look at that, three for three."

Smiling, she led the way to the opposite side of the courtyard. Sterling could feel eyes on them, but he hoped those would fade away after they sat down. They angled their chairs close together. "What's new with the old gang? Tell me what you know," Sterling commanded.

Reminiscing was safe and equal footing for both of them. Bess began to talk about people they knew, and Sterling found himself relaxing as he watched her. She was pretty, even with age, even with whatever was weighing her down. It had been a long time since he let down his guard, since he reached out and touched a pretty girl, just because he could. After Duncan cheated with Chelsea, Sterling swore off women for a while. He reached out now, extending his fingers and let them slide down her bicep. Bess smiled, but her glance flitted uncertainly away. Sterling paused, considering. Was the uncertainty genuine or practiced on her part? He had always liked a challenge. Bess knew, and she had always known how to present herself as one, to keep him interested, usually by playing him off other guys. But there were no other guys around now. No one had approached them and tried to become part of their circle. Seemingly everyone else was off talking or possibly paired off. Sterling didn't bother to look. All he knew was that he and Bess were alone in their cozy corner and the feeling of déjà vu weighed heavily against him. Bess was all at once familiar and something completely new. It would be so easy.

They talked for a while longer and then, when temptation reared its head again, Sterling didn't fight it. He was tired of fighting against everything that felt good, tired of feeling numb, tired of the gnawing weight of anxiety. Tonight he wanted one good thing; he wanted Bess. He breached the distance between them, pressing his lips to hers, asking for a response without using words. The hesitancy was there again. For a millisecond, Bess held herself in check, then her hand reached up to rest on his chest and she leaned invitingly into him. His hand slid to her waist, and suddenly he was being ripped off her and tossed mercilessly to the ground.

Dazed, he hopped to his feet and prepared to fight. Hogue towered over him in a rage. "What's your problem?" Sterling shouted.

"You want to know my problem, Sterling?" Hogue returned, cold fury in his voice. "I'll tell you my problem. You're kissing my wife."

CHAPTER 4

The night couldn't possibly get worse, so of course it did.

"What?" Sterling exclaimed. "You're married? To each other?" How had he missed that? How had Duncan missed it? Or had Duncan known and failed to tell him? It would be like him not to pass on pertinent information.

"No," Bess said. Where Hogue's tone had been thunderous, hers sounded resigned, tired.

"Yes until it's official," Hogue angrily amended.

"When did you get married?" Sterling asked.

"About two weeks after I found out I was pregnant, ten years ago," Bess said.

"You have a kid?" Sterling said, his tone softer now, even though his throat felt like he'd swallowed sand.

"Three," Hogue said, and his tone hadn't softened.

"Three," Sterling repeated, almost staggering under the weight of the knowledge. Three kids by the age of twenty eight and married a decade. He faced Hogue who seemed to be waiting to see what he would do with the new information. "I'm sorry. I didn't know. If I'd have known, I wouldn't have touched her."

"Wouldn't you?" Hogue asked, his tone deadly.

"What?" Sterling replied.

"Hogue," Bess warned.

Hogue shrugged one shoulder. "It seems to me you came here with a purpose tonight. If not Bess, then what?"

"I didn't come here with a purpose," Sterling argued.

"Why did you come here?" Hogue pressed. "You disappear for ten years, not a word to anybody but Duncan in all that time, and then you show up here tonight. Did you miss being the conquering hero? Did you need the adulation of your adoring fans and my wife?"

Hogue was half drunk. Sterling shouldn't let the words bother him, but they did, settling under his skin like a handful of well-placed sea urchins. His fuse was too short lately, his self-control lacking, his temper at the ready. "Why do you think I came?" he exploded. "Why did any of us come? Because Alby called and asked us to, because we felt sorry for her and ashamed of the idea of staying away."

"You showed up after a ten year absence because you felt sorry for Alby?" Hogue said, incredulous.

"Didn't everybody?" Sterling thought of the way Alby had scuttled around all night, serving everyone, playing hostess, trying to set them all at ease while as far as he could tell everyone had ignored her or tried to. Had anyone even thanked her? She was so *good*, so utterly righteous. They didn't deserve her, and yet she was like an unwanted dog, trying to sidle close for attention and never losing heart, despite being repeatedly shoved away. "She's little more than a lapdog, an unwanted pest in her own home."

The way everyone froze, he knew. He knew he had shouted the words and Alby heard them. He turned to look and locked eyes with her. Two little spots of color stood out on her cheeks, in contrast to her pale face.

"Alby," he croaked, extending his hand toward her.

She turned and walked away, went inside the house, and closed the door.

There was a moment of silence, and then Hogue laughed. "Don't know what I was worried about. Guess the old suave Sterling is dead. Long live his evil new replacement." He turned and ambled off with

Reams and Stokes, his earlier fury dissolved in the wake of Sterling's monumental blunder. Bess remained. The little spark of attraction he'd felt for her was gone now, dampened forever by the knowledge that she was Hogue's wife, however temporary, that she'd born him three children.

"You should probably go after her," Bess said, surprising him not only with her words by with her soft tone. Bess had always been the instigator in the let's-be-cruel-to-Alby game, never the savior or protector.

"Let me see a picture of your kids," Sterling demanded, a distraction from the oncoming humiliation of seeing Alby. He had never lashed out so cruelly before, and especially not to someone so soft and unprotected. Sterling had always stuck up for Alby, always inserted himself between her and whatever meanness she encountered in his view. He'd hated the way kids had made her an easy target and hadn't allowed it to happen, whenever he could help it. It was something he had prided himself on, the fact that he'd been her secret and silent protector. And now he'd been the one to humiliate her, publicly and in her own home. He felt sick all the way to his heart that he'd hurt her, someone so underserving of his wrath.

Bess pulled out her phone and handed it over with a little smile, a mixture of love and pride he was unused to seeing on her face. Sterling took the phone and stared at it. The oldest was a boy, a big, hulking bruiser.

"He looks exactly like Hogue."

"He's not," Bess declared. "He's sweet and soft and sensitive." Sterling wondered how it went over with Hogue that his son was tenderhearted, but Bess's tone told him all he needed to know. Her son's temperament was a source of stress and anxiety between husband and wife. Next was a little girl who, though adorable, was clearly the tomboy of her father's dreams. Finally there was a toddler whose sex he couldn't determine, but he or she was young enough to make Sterling smile. He had always liked little ones.

"Wow," Sterling said, handing the phone back. "Congratulations."

"Thank you," Bess said, sliding her finger lovingly over the picture on the phone before tucking it away.

"Any chance you and Hogue will work things out?" he asked.

She let out a breath. "I don't think so, Sterling. You know what he's like."

He did. Hogue hadn't done much to expel the chowderhead image of football players. He'd been big and tough and mean, picking on anyone and everyone he deemed smaller or weaker. He'd loved to win at all costs and hadn't cared who got in his way. Still, there had to be some good in there, didn't there? "I bet that little girl has him wrapped."

Bess smiled. "She does."

Sterling paused. "I bet you do, too."

She paused also, her look turning sad again. "I used to."

He gave her shoulder a quick pat, cognizant now that Hogue was likely watching. He faced the house. "I guess I'd better suck it up and make amends."

"Take heart, Alby never stays mad at anybody," Bess said. Her tone was fond. Sterling turned to her in surprise again.

"Are you and Alby friends now?"

She shrugged and shook her head. "My oldest is a lot like Alby. It's given me a better understanding. He's sweet and kind, and so is she." It was hard to tell in the darkness, but she looked like she might be blushing, as if the newfound tenderness for Alby embarrassed her. Or maybe she was remembering all the times she hadn't been kind to Alby, all the times she'd made Alby the butt of her jokes.

Bess was lost in her own world now, and there was nothing more to say anyway. Sterling forced his feet to turn toward the house, plodding as he made his way to Alby. He expected to find her in the kitchen, working like usual as if nothing had happened. But she wasn't. He wandered to the bedroom she'd taken him to earlier and tried the door. It was locked. He knocked.

"Yes," she said. Her voice was soft and tremulous, and guilt knifed through him. At the same time, he was slightly annoyed by her timid passivity. Why couldn't she have yelled at him, screamed at him, told him he was a horrible jerk who was intruding on her hospitality? Bess would have. Anyone normal would have. Why did Alby have to be such a doormat all the time? It frustrated him, but frustration wasn't exactly what he should be going for when he needed to make amends.

"Alby, it's Sterling."

There was no answer, and the door remained closed.

"Could you open up, please?" he asked.

"No."

He blinked at the door in surprise. To his knowledge, it was the first time Alby had ever said no to him or probably to anyone else. She was always at the ready, always helpful and obedient.

"Please? I need to talk to you."

"Go away, Sterling." Her tone wasn't vehement or demanding. It was still polite and soft, but she didn't say please. For Alby, that was a big deal, he reckoned.

"I'd like to talk to you, to apologize."

"No, thank you."

He blinked at the door. "You're not going to let me apologize?"

There was no answer, and now he was becoming frustrated, and he was becoming frustrated that he was becoming frustrated. Alby couldn't even accept an apology like normal people. "So, what, I'm supposed to linger in guilt forever?"

There was no answer. He almost kicked the door, but he forced himself to calm down. Maybe this was how Alby resolved any sort of hurt or anger. It wasn't as if he knew her. Maybe she would absorb the hurt and go back to pretending it hadn't hurt; that had been her M/O in high school. Bess's barbs had seemingly bounced off her. She had seemed impervious to any taunts on their part. Sterling remained at the closed door a moment longer, then he turned and went home, not bothering to say goodbye to anyone outside.

Duncan was already in the car, waiting for him.

"Don't say a word," Sterling growled.

"I wouldn't dare," Duncan replied, but he didn't have to. After so many years of being best friends, they could read each other in silence. Now, for instance, Duncan's face showed its surprise at Sterling's outburst. And that it had been directed toward Alby. But it wasn't his shock that upset Sterling; it was his glee. Sterling had always been the beloved golden boy, the one who could do no wrong while Duncan had stumbled through life, self-centered and wreaking havoc. Now the tables were turned and he was thrilled to see Sterling knocked off his horse. And what hurt the most was that Sterling deserved his censure. *Be best.* What a joke. Irate with Duncan, with himself, with the world in general, he crossed his arms and stared out the window, silent and sullen all the way home.

CHAPTER 5

he next morning when Sterling's phone rang, he was still asleep. Since having a breakdown and being diagnosed with depression, he had slipped into all manner of bad habits. Staying up too late and sleeping in being chief among them. Being disciplined about anything seemed like an added weight on top of all the work he was already doing to keep the sadness and anxiety at bay. And it wasn't like he had a bustling business to get to. His store opened at ten. He'd be lucky if one customer came in before noon. He reached for his phone without checking the ID and said a groggy hello.

"This is Sharon Preston. I'm with the Human Resources department at Irving Corporation. Someone gave me your name as a possible candidate for one of our positions, and I'm calling to schedule an interview."

Sterling sat up, trying hard to blink the sleep from his eyes and brain. He cleared his throat. "Yes, I'm available." *Boy, am I available. You have no idea how available I am.* His eyes scanned the interior of his boyhood room with a squint.

"Excellent. Would this afternoon work for you?"

Sterling thought fast. He'd have to compile a resume and references, but surely he could have it ready if he got started on it now. "Yes, thank you."

"Perfect." They set a time. Sharon was about to hang up when Sterling added a question.

"Can I ask who gave you my name?"

"Alby," Sharon replied, and the knife of guilt that was still in Sterling's chest shifted a little deeper. He tossed his phone aside and lay down. Alby had given the HR woman his name for the job, even though he'd hurt her immensely. Did that mean she forgave him? Sterling gave a little shake of his head, feeling both grateful and peeved. He had almost admired the glimpse of backbone he'd witnessed last night when he tried to apologize. But apparently Alby was the same old doormat.

Pushing aside thoughts of Alby, Sterling stretched and then set aside the covers and sat up. He needed to shave, shower, and work on his resume, in that order. But first, coffee.

A few hours later, he arrived at Irving Corp, Alby's father's company. It had been an almost immediate success, transforming seemingly overnight into the town's biggest and best employer. They paid well and provided generous benefits and incentives. The company was still family owned, despite the fact that they had branches now in four other states. As a young man, Alby's innovative father had discovered a way to make asphalt paving faster, more durable, and cheaper. It had been a game changer, and he held the patent on the technology, meaning that every time someone paved with asphalt, Alby's family received a cut of the profits. They were ridiculously wealthy and Sterling was practically salivating over the chance to work for them. Money. Benefits. A retirement account. All of the things that hadn't mattered when he started his shop now suddenly felt vitally important as he zoomed toward thirty without a penny to his name.

Still, he held himself in check, not wanting to appear as desperate as he really was. He hadn't had a lot of jobs since college, had worked for himself the last six years, a fact that became readily apparent during his interview.

"I have several candidates for this job who have experience in project management. Tell me why I should hire you among them," Peter Stultz, Alby's cousin and second in command at the company, said.

It was the sort of question Sterling dreaded. He had spent the morning wracking his brain, trying to find an answer. "I have leadership experience, both on the football field and in my personal life. I know the kind of grit and determination it takes to get a job done, but I try always to do it with a smile, not lording my leadership over those under my command." That part was true. Sterling had always been well liked by others; people had always looked up to him as a leader. Why, he had no idea, but they did. And he had tried never to take advantage of that, until yesterday when he yelled mean things about Alby for no reason. She wasn't in today's meeting, and he was glad. It was her company, so she might have been. But he had no idea what her function was in the company. Knowing her, he couldn't guess it would be much. What could she reasonably do? Flit around the company offering to serve everyone sweet tea and cheese straws?

They talked for a while longer. The questions felt grueling and intense, but maybe it was because Sterling was so far out of touch with the working world. In fact, he realized with a start, this was his first interview. He'd put in applications and resumes all over the place, but all he had to put in the employment history was "store owner," and at most places, that wasn't enough.

So now he would sit on pins and needles and wait. In the meantime, he decided to see if he could find Alby and make amends. He left Peter's office and turned right.

"May I help you?" a woman asked. By her demeanor and desk placement, he realized she was a secretary.

"Hi, I'm here to see Alby," he said. The woman's eyes were narrowed speculatively on him, and he tried not to squirm.

"Did you have an appointment?"

He almost laughed at that. An appointment with Alby? Did anyone actually make an appointment to see Alby? "Uh, no."

The woman's lips pursed.

"I'm an old friend," he added, and the judgmental lips softened slightly.

"Whom may I tell her is here?"

"Sterling Mathew Thompson," he said, using his full name in deference to the woman's formality. He sat uninvited and waited for the woman to buzz Alby. He pictured Alby in her office, likely working on a cross stitch or maybe knitting a blanket for premies at the hospital. That was something she had actually done once. He remembered Bess making fun of her for it, though why an act of kindness should be an object of ridicule, he had no idea.

"A Sterling Mathew Thompson to see you, ma'am," the secretary said, and Sterling blinked at her. Alby was a ma'am to someone? Wonders never ceased.

"No," Alby said.

The secretary faced him with something like satisfaction. "I'm sorry, unfortunately Ms. Mowry can't fit you in her schedule today. I could try to make an appointment, but the next few days are booked."

Sterling stood. "No, thank you. I'll try her at home." He had no idea why he added that last part, almost peevishly, except that this woman had somehow set Alby above him and it grated on his nerves. True, Alby owned the company, but it was *Alby*.

The secretary didn't reply or even glance at him again. It was as if he had been summarily dismissed from her presence at the knowledge that he wasn't good enough to see her boss. And now Sterling would find a way to make Alby see him, if only to prove to himself he could. The town was small, and this was Alby. How long could she reasonably avoid him?

A while, as it turned out. When he arrived at her house that night, he found it dark. Of course it was possible she was still avoiding him, but the house looked and seemed empty. He sat on the porch for a while, waiting, but eventually gave up. Where did Alby go? What did she do with her time? He couldn't imagine.

The next morning he showed up early with a latte he'd brought for her from their town's lone coffee shop. Her door was answered by a middle aged woman, and Sterling blinked in surprise.

"May I help you?" the woman asked.

"I'm here to see Alby," Sterling replied, feeling like a kid meeting a date's mother. This wasn't Alby's mother, however. Sterling knew Alby's parents, had known them for years before they died.

"One moment, please," the woman said, and the door clicked softly into place as she turned her back on him. Sterling waited, feeling oddly annoyed, and then she returned. "I'm sorry, Miss Mowry is busy at the moment. May I take a message?"

Sterling sighed and handed the woman the latte. "No, but tell her I brought a peace offering."

The woman blinked at the drink a moment and then nodded. Sterling turned and drove away, the gnawing sense of annoyance now combined with exasperation. Alby had a secretary *and* a housekeeper. As he rounded the bend beside her house, a new thought occurred to him. He'd follow her and force a conversation when she arrived at work. He pulled his car to the side of the road and waited. Twenty minutes later, Alby's car rounded the bend, but Alby wasn't in the driver's seat. *She has a driver?* Apparently so, and he didn't park the car in the lot. He paused at the turnaround by the front door and opened the door for Alby. She stepped smiling from the back seat and rested her hand on his, no doubt thanking him. He beamed at her, said something, and they parted ways.

The driver watched her until she was in the building, and then a few seconds after that. Sterling shifted uncomfortably. The driver was young. Was it possible he had designs on Alby? Or rather, her money? It was impossible for him to imagine anyone actually being attracted to Alby. Not that she was ugly. She had a pretty face and a passable figure, but she was so *there.* There was absolutely nothing that stood out about her. She was one of those people who, unless you made a specific study of her face, was utterly forgettable. She could play the extra in every Hollywood movie and no one would notice that it was the same person on repeat.

He resigned himself to the fact that Alby was wilier and more self-preserving than he gave her credit for. He would try to contact her again tomorrow, sure it would bring success. In the meantime, he had a failing store to try and salvage.

CHAPTER 6

The next day did not bring success, nor the next day, nor the day after that. For two solid weeks, Alby avoided him entirely, something Sterling would previously have thought impossible to do in his small town. In the interim, he got the job at her company. On the one hand he felt certain he would be able to track her down and fix the situation once they were in the same place day after day. On the other hand, he somehow knew he wouldn't. No doubt about it, Alby was avoiding him and doing a bang up job.

"What's wrong with you?" His cousin Taylor sat in the living room of his mother's house absently strumming on a guitar. Taylor had moved in when Birdie moved out, for reasons Sterling still wasn't clear on, something about a roommate situation gone bad in Atlanta. Their mothers were sisters and the two families had always been close, the kind of close you are when both living in the same tiny town. Clannish, to use the proper word. Taylor had been more like a little brother to both him and Birdie and while that had equaled a friendship on Birdie's part, to Sterling the kid had always been a bit of an annoyance. Not only was he five years younger and always in the way, but they were polar opposites. Except now, both adults and living under the same roof, Taylor was turning out to be another surprise. Previously the two had had nothing in common. They still didn't, but Sterling found he didn't mind so much anymore. Blood actually was turning out to be thicker than water, at least in their case.

"I got a job," Sterling said.

"You don't look happy about it. Where's it at?"

"Project manager at Irving Corp."

Taylor stopped strumming. "What? How'd that happen?"

Sterling shrugged. "Alby, I think."

"You know Alby?" Taylor said, sitting up in surprise.

"Sure, you know that. She was part of my friends group, back in the day."

Taylor gave him a look. Back then the two cousins hadn't paid a bit of attention to each other's lives. The fact that they were five years apart was a factor, but it was mostly their personalities that set them apart. Sterling had always excelled at everything, sports, academics, popularity. Taylor had hated school and people and found his solace in music and video games. It was only since Sterling returned home that they began to set aside those differences and bond. A new thought occurred to Sterling.

"How do *you* know Alby?"

Taylor shrugged, staring at the far wall. "I met her a while back at a show. She's nice."

Sterling's jaw dropped. "You have a crush on Alby."

Taylor rolled his eyes. "I'm twenty four years old; I don't have a *crush* on anybody. She's sweet and cute and, I don't know, there's something about her. She's different."

"That she is," Sterling agreed.

"Why do you say it like that?" Taylor asked.

His cousin was aggravatingly perceptive. "I sort of yelled at her when I was at her house a couple of weeks ago."

Taylor set aside the guitar that was going slack in his fingers. "You were at her house? And you yelled at her? That's like yelling at a baby mouse."

"I know, all right. I've been feeling bad about it, but she won't let me apologize." He ground the heels of his hands into his eye sockets.

"Won't let you apologize? What's that mean?"

"It means she's dodging me. She won't take my calls, won't see me, runs the other way when she sees me coming."

Taylor chuckled and reached for his guitar. "Oh, man."

"Oh, man, what?" Sterling snapped. His fuse was nonexistent lately. He took a breath and tried to push back his too-eager temper.

"Oh, man, it's funny that the first woman you can't get is Alby."

"I'm not trying to *get* her; I'm trying to apologize to her. I acted horribly, and I feel awful. It's just…Alby. She's so…" He shook his head, uncertain how to explain. His cousin hadn't been popular; he wouldn't understand the dynamics.

"What? Kind? Rich? Well respected?"

Sterling quirked an eyebrow. "Alby? Well respected?"

Taylor rolled his eyes and set aside the guitar again. "Hold on, I'll show you something." He went to his room and returned a moment later with a magazine from Atlanta. Alby's face adorned the cover. Sterling reached for it, blinking in surprise as he read the caption. "Humanitarian of the year. Alby?"

Taylor nodded.

Sterling set down the magazine. "So she gave a bunch of money to stuff. Lots of rich people give money away."

Taylor shook his head and reached for the magazine, opening it this time. Sterling saw picture after picture of Alby, an apron tied around her waist as she served the homeless Thanksgiving. A picture of her in scrubs as she held sick babies at the hospital, surrounded by a group of rescue dogs she personally bought and dispersed to needy families, along with a year's supply of food and veterinary care, a park where she routinely weeded flowers and collected trash.

"Georgia's very own Mother Theresa," he muttered.

Taylor ripped the magazine away. "Why do you have to say it like that?"

"Like what?" Sterling asked in surprise at Taylor's vehement tone.

"Like Alby's defective for being nice," Taylor said.

"I don't know," Sterling said, running his hands through his hair, disheveling it. "I don't *know*. It's just…in high school, she was kind of our whipping boy, you know? The person who was always there, always tagging along, siphoning our popularity. She was and still is a doormat, and it drives me crazy for reasons I can't articulate. I didn't even know it made me angry until I saw her doing it again, after all this time. Why does she? Why does she hang around a group of people who don't like her, who are actively mean to her, and beg for scraps of our affection? It's maddening, and it makes me mad."

"But why does it make you mad at her? It should make you mad at you and all your other friends for being such heartless jerks," Taylor said.

"It does," Sterling agreed adamantly. "It makes me feel like the worst sort of person, and I think that's what makes me so mad because it's been ten years. How can I still be this person who willingly treats another human being that way? So I've been trying to track her down, to apologize and make it right, but she won't let me, and now she's going to be my boss and I'm basically wallowing in misery and guilt every second of the day."

Taylor was grinning at him, enjoying the misery, but Sterling supposed he had a right. It hadn't been easy to be the unathletic little cousin of the town's superstar athlete. Comparisons had likely been made, unspoken and out loud. Sterling had heard them a few times. *What sport do you play, Taylor? I don't, ma'am; I play guitar.*

"It's possible I could help you," Taylor said, his smile telling him he would continue to enjoy Sterling's misery for as long as possible, probably forever.

"How?"

"Alby comes to my shows sometimes," Taylor said.

Sterling scowled. It was obvious to him that his cousin had a crush on Alby. Did Alby return the sentiment? That would be odd, to say the least. Alby might view him as a big brother, but he had never seen her as a little sister. "Why?"

"Because she's nice that way and, hold your shock, because my band is good and lots of people come to hear us," Taylor said.

Sterling refrained from rolling his eyes as well as from telling

Taylor the odds on making it as a band. Let the kid learn the hard lessons for himself. "Okay," he said instead.

Taylor relaxed slightly, as if he had been bracing himself for an argument or unsolicited advice, which he probably had. "We have a gig this weekend. I could call and invite her."

"Do it," Sterling hastened.

Taylor pulled out his phone and hit a button. *He has Alby on speed dial, apparently,* he noted in some absent part of his brain, not sure why it should bother him, except he was the one who had known Alby for twenty three years and didn't even have her number. "Hey, Alby, it's Taylor," Taylor said, unnecessarily since Alby undoubtedly had his name programed in her phone as well. "I have a thing this weekend, and I was wondering if you'd like to come."

Sterling couldn't hear her words, but her tone sounded delighted, and he rolled his eyes. Sure, for his cousin she was agreeable. Then again Taylor hadn't yellingly insulted her in front of all her friends, but why quibble over details?

"Excellent," Taylor said, smiling. "It's out of town, about an hour away. I was thinking maybe you could ride with Sterling."

Alby's tone changed immediately and she began to backpedal. "Mmm, hmm, mmm, hmm," Taylor said, nodding. He pulled the phone away and mouthed to Sterling, *"Whoa, what did you do to her?"*

Sterling reached for the phone and yanked it from his fingers. "Alby, stop this, you're being ridiculous. Stop avoiding me and let me…" The phone was dead.

"Well, that failed miserably," Taylor said, and then mimed a bomb exploding. Sterling sank back to the couch and tossed Taylor his phone. *Now what?*

"Here's what you're going to do. You're going to text her in a few days and tell her it was all a ruse, that I was only going if she was going to go and now I'm not. Invite her again, tell her you're certain I won't go," Sterling directed.

Taylor studied him. "You want me to lie to Alby?"

"Bald faced and outrageously," Sterling agreed.

Taylor picked up his phone with a sigh. "Fixing you up with the girl I like—maybe I'm the one who should get the humanitarian award."

"It's not like that with me and Alby," Sterling assured him.

Taylor fixed his eyes on him with a frown. "It's you. It's always like that."

"Ladies love Sterling, what can I say?"

"Not that," Taylor replied and began once again strumming his guitar.

CHAPTER 7

*S*terling knew nothing about music, but even he recognized that Taylor and his band were talented and, true to his word, they had something of a following. At least people had cheered when their names were called to take the stage. If not for his gnawing anxiety, he might have settled back and enjoyed the show, might even have tried to pick up one of the girls who sat adoringly staring at his cousin. Maybe for once he could have used his cousin as a pickup line. *I'm with the band, that's my cousin.* The fact that the girl would have wanted him for that reason and that reason alone wouldn't have been enough to deter him, but Alby was. He had been hiding, waiting for her to make an appearance, for the last hour. Just when he believed she wouldn't show, she did, slipping into the back and staring warily around as if she were a burglar when in reality Sterling knew it was because of him. She was checking to make sure he was nowhere around before she relaxed and enjoyed the show. He let her do so, watching her expression soften into a smile before making his move. Did she actually like Taylor? As in *like him* like him? He realized the direction of his thoughts and rolled his eyes. He wasn't certain he had wondered that about a girl since high school, and certainly it had never applied to his little cousin. Who Taylor liked or dated hadn't concerned him a whit until now. But it would be weird if Taylor dated Alby, wouldn't it? Alby was his friend. Or she had been, up until a few weeks ago when he crushed her heart and ruined things between them, possibly forever.

With that thought in mind, he stepped out of his hiding place and sat down at her table. She glanced at him with an absent smile, did a double take, and stood to go.

"Nope," Sterling said. He grasped her arm and ushered her to a hallway by the bathrooms. The door closed. Music still filtered out, but it was quiet now, as if someone had hit the mute button.

"Let me go, Sterling," Alby demanded, trying to tug her arm free of his grasp.

In answer, he stepped closer, pinning her to the wall with his body. She blinked up at him in surprise, but he was feeling a bit of shock of his own. He hadn't meant to do that, to press his body to hers so completely. If he had thought about it, he would have done it anyway because this was Alby and feeling attraction for her would be like feeling attraction for milk. But then he did feel a spark, and he wasn't sure what to do with the feeling. *It's been way, way too long since I had a date if Alby is having this effect on me,* was his first thought, followed closely by, *she feels and smells better than anyone in recent memory.*

Belatedly he realized Alby was staring up at him in question while he remained blank and silent, shocked at his actions and response to them.

"Stop avoiding me," he decreed, aiming to regain the upper hand.

"Stop chasing me," she countered, cute upturned nose wrinkling slightly.

"I'm not," he insisted.

Her eyebrows rose and his lowered. This was *Alby.* She wasn't supposed to counter him or make him feel like a stupid kid for his fruitless pursuit of her.

"I just want to apologize," he said.

"Fine, go ahead."

He took a breath. He should start from high school and apologize for all the wrong things that had ever happened to her on his watch, for allowing her at any time to be a target. Then he should move on to his own recent screwup and grovel for forgiveness. "Sorry," was what he eventually mumbled. *Smooth, moron.*

A hint of a smile tugged at her lips. "You're bad at this."

He smiled full bore. "Yes, I am. But I'm also sorry. Really sorry. What I said was totally uncalled for and inappropriate. I should never have said it."

"I notice you didn't say it was untrue," Alby murmured.

He opened his mouth to…what? Contradict? Say that, no, of course she wasn't a doormat they had all taken advantage of. He couldn't; they would both know he was lying. His hand reached up to brush the stray hairs off her face, gentle, tender. He tried to make his tone the same. "The words might have had some truth, but the anger and unkindness had nothing to do with you. I *like* you, Alby; I've always liked you. It was me I was mad at, and maybe a little bit Hogue and Bess."

"You really didn't know they were married?" she asked, squinting at him incredulous.

He scowled and shook his head. "I would never have kissed her if I'd known."

"No, that didn't seem like you. But it's been ten years. Maybe you've changed." She seemed to be talking more to herself than him.

"Maybe I have, but I'm not the kind of man who makes a move on a married woman."

"Well, that's a relief," she said, but she didn't sound relieved. She sounded hurt and sad.

"Do you forgive me?" he pressed, ducking slightly to catch her eye.

"Of course I do," she said in the same listless tone. He inspected her. She gazed away from his scrutiny, her eyes skittering to a spot on the far wall.

"It doesn't seem like it," he said. Was Alby a pouter? He had no idea. He touched his finger under her chin, directing her eyes back to his. They were filled with pain, and he felt something within him crumple a little. Alby was so little and harmless; she should never feel such pain.

"Forgiveness doesn't change the fact that the words are true, Sterling. I've known, I've always known how much I didn't fit in. And I always knew everyone else knew, but no one ever said the words out loud before. And now, I can't unhear them." She shook her head as if trying to push the hurtful words away, his hurtful words. Sterling felt awful, like the worst sort of bully.

"Why did you do it?" he asked the question he had always wanted to ask. Why had Alby trailed after them all these years, soaking up crumbs of their affection?

"Because as much as I didn't fit in, it was the closest I came to fitting in. My family was rich and employed almost everyone's parents, that excluded me from being friends with most everyone else in town. Don't you think I tried? Don't you think I tried to hang out with the math kids, the drama kids, the music kids, *anyone* who would accept me? But none of them did and, for them, I had nothing to offer. At least with you all I had a cool place to party and hang out, somewhere with a pool and a game room dark enough for making out. And sometimes it seemed like fitting in, it seemed like friendship, if I closed my eyes and squinted real hard." Tears filled her eyes, and she blinked them away, still staring hard at the far wall.

"We are real friends," Sterling heard himself say.

Now when she looked at him it was with something like annoyance, the first time he'd ever seen such an emotion on her face. Not to say it had never been there before, but he had never paid much attention to her feelings. Or her face. Now as he studied it, it was prettier than he remembered. And there was another startling realization to add to his growing collection: Alby was kind of adorable. "Come on, Sterling. You're the team captain, and I'm the team manager. We are not friends."

He smiled. "No, Alby, you're the owner of the company and I'm your employee, but we are still friends. And from now on we'll be real friends, ones who talk and exchange information."

"What kind of information?" she asked.

"I hate peaches," he threw out.

Her jaw dropped on an affronted gasp. "You live in the Peach State."

"Don't tell the authorities," he said, leaning close to whisper.

She smiled, the first real smile she'd shown him, and he eased his arms around her. Until this point they had been pressed together, their arms dangling helplessly at their sides. It was a relief to have something to do with his hands, and her waist felt nice, small and well toned.

"Now your turn," he prompted. "Tell me something."

"Last year I got arrested."

He froze. "Say again."

"Last year I went to North Carolina. It was summer. I saw a dog in a hot car, looking like it would soon breathe its last. So I picked up a rock, bashed the back window, and saved the dog."

"You got arrested for that?"

She nodded. "Also because when the owner came out and confronted me, we got into it."

He pressed his lips together. "What were the charges?"

"Destruction of property and disorderly conduct."

His mouth was hanging open, but he couldn't seem to help it. He had never so much as heard Alby raise her voice.

"My lawyer got the charges dropped, but I was still booked, still taken to jail. There's a mug shot out there somewhere." She pressed her lips together. "I should not have told you that. Don't tell anyone, please."

He laughed. "I won't. And no one would believe me, if I did."

Someone opened the door to the hallway and skirted by them. Music filtered out. Alby glanced that way. "We should get back. Taylor's going to think we abandoned him."

Sterling's amusement fled. "Do you have a crush on my cousin?"

"He's only twenty four," Alby said.

"That wasn't a no," Sterling pointed out.

"I guess it wasn't," Alby said. She put up her hands and gave his chest a light shove, squirming out of his embrace. Sterling took a step back and they returned to the other room together.

CHAPTER 8

*A*fter the apology, Sterling felt better. With absolution, he had expected a return to the status quo, meaning he would go back to forgetting about Alby, but she didn't make it possible.

For one thing, they actually had fun during the remainder of their evening. After he finished his set, Taylor sat with them. Sterling sat back, observing Alby and his cousin for signs of mutual attraction. They certainly seemed taken with each other, but he couldn't tell if it was attraction or merely friendship. Did Alby know how to flirt? Doubtful.

"Why are you staring at us like we're in a science experiment?" Taylor demanded after a half hour of monopolizing the conversation.

"I'm taking it all in," Sterling said.

"Taylor, you were fantastic. Did I mention?" Alby gushed.

"You did, in fact," Sterling reminded her.

"It can't be said enough," Taylor said. "Or by enough people."

Sterling huffed. "Yes, you're super talented. We're all basking in your glory."

"There's the stuff," Taylor said. The other band finished, and it was time for his second set. Alby watched him go with a fond smile.

"He's sweet," she said.

Sterling watched her, still unable to get a read on her level of interest in his cousin. "Have you ever kissed anyone?" he blurted.

Alby's cheeks warmed. He was certain she'd say no, so it came as something of a surprise when she didn't. "Yes, a, uh, few times."

"Who?" Sterling pressed, leaning forward with interest.

She shook her head.

"Come on, Alby, fess up."

"Why? Why should I tell you?" she asked. Her nose wrinkled in annoyance again and he had to push back a smile. He liked to annoy Alby, he realized. He shouldn't, but it was so much better than the bland Alby of his memory. Alby was a real person with real feelings and—dare he believe it—a passionate nature.

"Because that's what friends do—we tell each other our embarrassing secrets."

"I already told you my embarrassing secret. I got thumb printed by a jailer named Bubba."

Sterling sputtered. "But you know my embarrassing secrets because you were part of them. I haven't done much stupid stuff since I left school. You, you're a mystery. Who have you been kissing, girl?"

"No one recent. It happened in high school." She stared hard at the stage.

Sterling scooted slightly closer. "Do tell."

She licked her lips and looked around to make sure no one was eavesdropping. "Hogue."

She couldn't have shocked him more than if she hit him over the head with a chair. "Hogue? The same Hogue who spent a night in the hospital after eating three bags of flaming hot Doritos on a dare?"

"Yes, but that didn't happen on a night we kissed," she said.

He leaned forward, earnestly imploring. "Spill because I sense a story."

She shrugged. "Junior year, Bess had been particularly mean and made me cry. Hogue came upon me unawares at a party. He sat down beside me and tried to comfort me. When that didn't work, he kissed me. After that we made out quite a few times, here and there and everywhere. The locker room, the band room, underneath the bleachers."

"Huh. I never would have guessed Hogue had it in him. Did you like him?"

"For a while I fancied myself in love with him. There's something about a bad boy, you know, and feeling like you might be the only one to see his tender side. I cried at his wedding, and then I put it all away."

"Because he was married?" Sterling guessed.

"Yes, because he was married and because it was time to grow up, to put away childish dreams. I started learning the ropes of the business soon after, and it seemed like the last whisper of being a kid."

"Hogue was mean to you," Sterling noted.

"Yeah, it was pretty messed up. He wouldn't acknowledge me in public, then in private he would tell me I was the only one who understood him. It was like he resented me for being attracted to me. For a while I had it in my head that we were Romeo and Juliet. I sort of gave up that notion when Romeo got another woman pregnant. Thrice."

"And now? Do you have any lingering designs on Hogue? Because, from the sounds of it, he's about to be single again."

"No," Alby said vehemently, shaking her head. "And I wouldn't give up on him and Bess too soon. There's a lot of history there. I think she actually is his Juliet."

"I used to think she was mine," Sterling admitted.

"Are you still hung up on Bess?" Alby asked, resting her hand comfortingly on his. He gave it a squeeze.

"Nah. I think I could be, if given half a chance. We have history, and she's pretty. I always liked her spunk and sass. But, as you said, she's a married woman. I have no desire to get involved in whatever that is."

"I've never had spunk or sass," Alby said. She withdrew her hands and sat on them.

"I don't know about that, jailbait. It's a sure bet Bess has never been arrested," Sterling said and watched her face bloom with a pleased flush. It was highly possible Alby had no idea the firebrand lying in wait inside her, and that was all kinds of intriguing to him. They spent the remainder of the evening talking and laughing, occasionally joined by Taylor when he wasn't on the stage. When the evening finished, Sterling followed her to make sure she got home okay. He drove away feeling…what? Relieved, undoubtedly. He'd hated knowing how deeply he'd hurt a gentle soul, one who had been especially undeserving of his wrath. More than that, he felt a bit surprised, both by his enjoyment of the evening and by Alby herself. She was as sweet as he remembered, but funnier, too. It was possible she had always been funny and easy to talk to and he'd never paid attention. Or maybe it was because she had always held herself in reserve with him, slightly awed by his status and popularity. He had been the king of their high school. Girls like Alby had given him a wide berth, too nervous and shy to talk to him. But after embarrassing himself monumentally in front of her, any sense of awe on her part was long gone. In a way he was relieved by that, but in another, he was rather depressed. He was shallow enough to admit he had always enjoyed her adulation. At the moment, he didn't have much else.

For the remainder of the weekend, Sterling didn't give Alby much thought. And then Monday rolled around. He had a monthly meeting with the other project managers and the head of the company who, he somehow didn't realize, was Alby. So great was his surprise he did an almost comedic double take when she breezed into the crowded conference room and sat at the head of the table. His gaze spread around the room at the other assembled people. Did any of them find it odd that Alby was in charge? If so, none of them showed it. They faced her attentively, pens at the ready to take notes.

"Good morning, everybody. Let's begin," Alby said. She didn't smile at him or make eye contact. Sterling might have thought she was purposely avoiding him so as not to show favoritism except that she was so focused on her agenda. Soon, after a moment of listening to her talk, Sterling came to a new and startling conclusion: Alby was actually in charge. It wasn't some joke or mistake. The girl who used to collect his sweaty towels in the locker room, blushing at the sight of so many jocks in their underwear, was now running a multi-million dollar company. Further, she was his boss, really and truly his boss.

Sterling had no idea why it took this long for it to sink in. Probably because he hadn't yet seen her in action until this morning. Before that, it had all seemed theoretical that Alby was in charge of everything, as if she was going through the motions of handling things but her cousin, Peter, was actually in charge. But, no, Alby was the one who handled the purse strings, and Peter was second in command. Sterling's sluggish brain remained bent on disbelief as he listened to her discuss every project with each manager, including progress, timeline, and budget. He was so enthralled with the new information that he almost forgot he would soon have to speak. All too soon, it was his turn.

"Sterling," Alby said, startling him.

"Hi," he blurted.

She bit back a smile. "Hi. How are you settling in? Is there anything we can do to make your job better?"

It was like Alby that she was the boss and still focused on his comfort but, unlike in their social lives, now her tone was tinged with authority and confidence. He found himself staring at her, mesmerized. "I'm fine, thank you. Everyone has been helpful. And as far as I can tell, the project is sticking to both its budget and its timeline."

"Excellent, thank you. Any other questions?"

One of the managers raised her hand. "Are you coming with us to Atlanta?"

Alby's expression closed. "No, Peter will be joining you."

Sterling noticed two of the managers exchange a glance. *I wonder what that's about.* The meeting was dismissed. Sterling hung back, hoping to catch a word with Alby, but she disappeared almost immediately. He meandered back to his office, still marveling over the fact that he had an actual office like a real grownup. With the salary he was being paid, he would soon be able to afford to move out of his mother's house again, possibly even to buy a house of his own. He could expand the bookshop's hours, hire another employee. Gratitude hadn't waned, even after the new began to wear off. He had been throwing himself into his job, attempting to be the best project manager on record, if only to prove to himself he was capable, not to mention as a repayment for Alby's kindness. And it had been kindness that got him the job. Regardless of the fact that she'd been angry and hurt, she had given his name to her hiring manager, guessing correctly how desperate he'd been for the job.

Before he could become lost in his work, he picked up his phone and dialed her extension. Her secretary answered and Sterling bit back his frustration. "Could I speak with Alby, please?"

"What is this in regard to?" Sandra asked. Sterling thought she took a little too much pleasure in her job as roadblock.

"Lunch," Sterling said.

"Hold, please," she said and then mindless piano music trilled in his ear for a second before she returned. "Ms. Mowry has an opening at one, if that will work with your schedule."

"That works just fine," Sterling said, his tone probably more terse than it should have been. *I've known Alby since kindergarten,* was what he actually wanted to say. *I shouldn't have to make an appointment with her like a stranger while you judge me for my forwardness.*

"It will be a working lunch in Ms. Mowry's office," Sandra warned.

"Perfect," Sterling said, and they disconnected.

He worked steadily until lunch, only stopping when his growling stomach reminded him of his meeting with Alby. He grabbed his sack lunch and headed toward her office, hoping against hope that Sandra was out. No such luck, though. She eyed him up and down, her gaze pausing on his lunch. He fought hard against the desire to hold his hands behind his back. She buzzed Alby to make sure he was allowed admittance and, reluctantly in Sterling's opinion, granted access.

Sterling paused on the threshold of Alby's office, scanning the interior. It was impressively large and well appointed. Alby sat behind a large mahogany desk in a buttery leather chair. Her head was down, staring at something on the desk in front of her. Sterling studied her, enjoying the way she gave whatever it was her rapt attention. Eventually she dragged her eyes away and looked up with a smile. "Hi, Sterling."

He sifted the greeting, checking for anything that might have changed in it since they said goodbye a few nights ago. There was nothing, though. She sounded as calm and friendly as ever, if a bit less shy. It was hard to maintain shyness and reserve after having someone's body pressed against yours for half an hour, however innocuous his intentions had been.

"Hi, Alby."

"Sit down, please. Oh, you brought your lunch. I had something catered." There was a knock on the door. A man entered with a cart and began arranging food.

Sterling gave a longsuffering sigh. "I suppose I could put away my hastily assembled peanut butter and jelly and eat this gourmet delight, if you insist on it."

"I insist," she said, smiling at his hungry expression. Whatever it was smelled amazing.

"You drive a hard bargain, Alby," he said, practically tossing his lunch away in his haste to reach for the plate of hot food that had been set before him. "How was the rest of your weekend?"

"Busy," she said.

He paused. Had Alby had a date? "With what?"

"Charity function on Saturday, church on Sunday, and then I played tennis."

"You play tennis?"

"I do, also golf."

"I stink at golf," he said.

"I highly doubt that," Alby replied.

"Why?"

"Because it's genetically impossible for you to be bad at sports. You've been programmed to be handsome, charming, and athletic. It's in your DNA."

"That didn't sound like a compliment," Sterling said.

"It wasn't," she said, smiling as she took a bite of her food.

"Wow," he mouthed, and she laughed. "Why aren't you going to Atlanta?"

She chewed, swallowed, wiped her mouth, and took a drink of water. "Because."

"Ah, informative. I completely understand."

She took a breath and twirled her drink between her fingers. "That stuff you said, about how it was in high school. That's how it still is, everywhere I go. I'm still that girl. I'll always be that girl."

Sterling shook his head. "No. I might have believed that, if I hadn't witnessed you in that meeting room a few hours ago. You were confident and in charge. Why can't you be like that in Atlanta?"

"Because I can't. Because they're all like you, like all our friends, born and imbued with whatever quirk of nature makes you popular by virtue of being alive. Even here, everyone is half in love with you. Do you know how many women I've heard commenting on the 'hot new project manager'?"

"No, but if you could write down a list of names, that would be great," Sterling said.

She ignored him and massaged her temples. "It's best if I don't involve myself in going places where I know I won't be accepted. At least if I stay here I have the illusion of being competent and in charge. I don't want my managers to see me as I was in high school. It was enough of a risk bringing you on."

He left his chair, went behind her desk, and perched on it. "Alby, come on."

"Come on what?" she asked, peering curiously at him.

"You are rich, pretty, kind, and intelligent. There is no reason for you to feel insecure. The other stuff, it takes some tweaking. You should go to Atlanta."

"Why?"

"Because I get the sense that something is up with your cousin."

She blinked at him in surprise. "Like what?"

He shrugged. "Something. There was an undercurrent when you said he'd be going in your stead. I haven't been here long enough to get a good read on the situation, but there's something there. This is me being your friend and telling you that for multiple reasons I think you need to do this."

"I don't think I can, Sterling. Especially not after having it put into words how people actually feel about me."

He picked up her hand and gave it a squeeze. "I think you should consider it."

"Why?"

He held onto her hand, making a study of her fingers as he spoke. "A few reasons. One, it bothers me, the way you are."

"So you've mentioned." She tried to tug her hand free, but he didn't relent.

"It does, though. It's a waste of a good woman. You have the potential to be so much more. My eyes have been opened to you, Albertine, and yours need to be, too. And it would be nice for me to have a friend there."

"I've been to these things before, with my dad when it was acceptable for me to tag along and observe. It's kind of a free for all, a total hookup scene. Are you sure you want me tagging along, standing in your way?"

"Who says you'd be in my way? I could totally work around you," he said, grinning.

"Gross." She tried to remove her hand, but once again he held fast.

"What I meant is that I am in no way interested in the free-for-all hookup scene. My life is currently being held together by safety pins. I have zero desire to add a woman into that mix."

"It looked like you were willing to add Bess into the mix the other night," she noted.

"A sign of my beleaguered mental state. Bess has always been high drama. If I'd been clear headed, I would have run away sooner."

She surprised him by reaching her free hand up to touch his cheek. "You worry me, Sterling."

"I worry myself sometimes, Alby," he returned. "All the more reason for you to come to Atlanta. It's my first work trip. I could use the advice and encouragement of my boss."

"Do you find it a bit ironic that I'm the boss, but you're all but demanding I tag along on a trip I arranged and am paying for?" she said.

"No. Quit stalling."

"I don't think I can do it; I'm not ready."

"You can do it. I'll get you ready," he said.

"What can you possibly do to get me ready?" she asked.

"Oh, you'll see," he said, his tone cryptic. He still held her hand. He brought it to his lips and bestowed a kiss, smiling when she regarded him with squinty skepticism.

CHAPTER 9

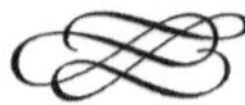

"$\mathcal{H}$ow does going out for pizza help get me ready to face high society?" Alby asked. It was Friday night and they sat in a booth at the town's lone pizza hangout, watching high schoolers coming and going. The sight made Alby reminiscent of when it had been them, and Sterling, too, apparently.

"Man, they look like babies," he said.

"They do, and you still haven't answered my question," she said.

"Patience, grasshopper. First we observe." They sat and watched the teenagers for a bit, giggling, flirting, laughing, talking. "Were we ever that young?"

"Some of us were," she said.

"How do you mean?" he asked.

"You always had an otherworldly maturity," she said.

He perked up in surprise. "I did?"

She nodded. "We all looked to you as our leader, as kind of a dad, I guess. You kept us in order, kept us in check. When kids got too mean to me, I always knew it was you who pulled them back."

"Huh," Sterling said. She made him sound different than he was, better and more level-headed. He wanted to ask her more, but they weren't here for him, they were here for her. "In every social group,

54

the players are always the same. The queen bee, that was Bess. The king."

"That was you," she said, poking him.

"The class clown," he continued.

"Hogue," she agreed.

"The hapless stooges."

"Reams and Stokes," she said.

"And sometimes the outsider, the one who doesn't quite belong," he said.

"Who would that have been?" she asked, feigning ignorance.

He gave her leg a squeeze. "Watch this group of kids and see if you can pick out their assigned roles."

Alby watched the kids a moment, sipping her tea so it didn't appear she was staring as blatantly as she was. The king and queen were obvious, both for their beauty and for their flagrant popularity. Activity swirled around them while they sat motionless, taking it all in as if it were being performed for their benefit, which it doubtless was. One kid was making walrus tusks out of two straws. His two friends were laughing at him, egging him on. Another kid sat half laughing, half staring longingly at Queen Bee. He was a bit quiet, a bit remote.

"Got it," she said.

"The quiet kid, is anyone watching him?" Sterling asked.

"No."

"He thinks everyone is. He feels like they're judging him, secretly making fun of him, wondering what he's doing with them when he so obviously doesn't fit in."

Alby squinted. "But no one is paying him a bit of attention. They're all focused on themselves."

"Exactly, Alby. The roles are always the same, and people are always thinking about themselves. Those are the two biggest take-aways I want you to have from this evening," Sterling said.

"I don't understand," Alby said.

"Once you know what to look for and who plays which role, it's easy to assimilate into any group. If you were a kid, you'd know to keep a wary eye out for the queen bee because she'd stick you as soon as your back was turned."

"Like Bess," Alby said.

"Just like Bess. And you'd know the goofy clown kid was going to find laughter at your expense at some point."

"Like Hogue."

"Like Hogue. When you know the players, when you realize how interchangeable they are, they become less intimidating. These people in Atlanta, they're not new or special or scary. They're merely Atlanta's version of Bess and Hogue and me and you."

"That does help a little, except I'm still the lonely outsider. Is that who I'll be in Atlanta?"

"No because they don't know that. They don't know that you're not our Bess. For all they know, you're the queen bee. And if I have anything to do with it, you will be."

"How?" she asked, a nervous little flutter in her stomach. Could he actually help her be something else? She desperately hoped so.

"Knowledge, understanding, practice, and acting," he said. "Can you tell what Queen Bee is thinking?"

"She's thinking she's cute and every boy there likes her."

He shook his head. "She's wondering if she's doing okay, she's wondering if they think she's too much, if they know how deeply she longs to be liked and accepted."

"How can you possibly know that?" Alby asked.

"Because it's what all of them are thinking; it's what everyone is thinking."

"You felt insecure?" Alby asked. To her, he had always been the epitome of cool. Handsome, popular, and self-assured.

"Alby, I still feel insecure. I'm a mess, a complete and total waste of space. But I don't let people know that. I act like I have it all together so people think I do. You wear your heart and your insecurity on your sleeve, and it's time to stop."

"But how do you stop?" she asked. "It's not like I want to act this way, like I want everyone to know what I'm thinking or feeling or how hard I'm trying or how much I want to be loved. I'm self-aware enough to realize it's not the right thing. But I also don't know how to fix it."

"You have to find your own coping mechanism. I take the Scarlet O'Hara approach: I won't think about it today, I'll think about it tomorrow, when I can stand it. Anytime something comes up, some fear or insecurity or certainty that I'm making a mess of everything, I push it aside and promise myself I'll deal with it later so I can keep my focus on the present situation. Bess uses her insecurity like a weapon, shooting arrows into other people, poking at their insecurity for her own amusement. Hogue makes everything a joke, figuring that if people are laughing at him to his face, they can't do it behind his back. I've heard your sense of humor from time to time. I would guess over the years you've stored up plenty of wry observations about us."

She shrugged, giving him a secret little smile.

"There," he said, pointing to her face. "That's your weapon. You're secretly making fun of us in your head."

"But it's not nice," she said.

He shrugged. "It's not about nice, it's about survival. When you feel yourself feeling insecure or starting to sink, conjure that smile and start silently picking people to pieces."

"I usually like to dwell on kind thoughts," she said.

"That's why you're being picked to pieces," he said. "You don't have to be mean, but you have to be self-protective. Find your humor shield, or they're going to eat you alive."

"This is a lot to take in," Alby said.

"I know," Sterling said.

"How do you know these things?"

"I don't know, I just know them," he said.

"I guess that's what makes you a natural leader, because you're good at understanding people and knowing how to make relationships work," she said. "When we're done fixing me, we should work on fixing you."

"What about me do you think needs fixed?" he asked, half joking. Though they were the same age, he had the feeling Alby had always looked up to him. To hear her say that he had issues was both an amusing and disturbing revelation.

"You always felt like you had a bigger purpose than the life you were living, bigger than this town, certainly. It's why you disappeared and opened the bookstore. But life hasn't been all it's supposed to be. You saw things, felt things you weren't prepared for. Now you're not sure how you're doing, and you don't know if working for me counts as failure."

His mouth opened, closed, and opened again. "Wow, Alby, strip me naked, why don't you?"

She grinned. "As it turns out, I've actually seen you naked. A few times."

"What?" he exclaimed.

"On Fridays in the locker room after practice, I used to do the laundry."

"I didn't know that," he said.

"No one did. Y'all walked around in your skivvies or less. It was quite the education."

"You could have said something. We would have covered up," he said.

"Now, where's the fun in that?" she asked.

He shook his head. "Wow, Alby, wow. You know what this means, don't you?"

"What?" she asked, reaching for her drink.

"I'm long overdue to see you naked," he said, and she spit her tea all over the table.

* * *

When they were finished with their pizza and conversation, Alby took him home. She had driven because she worked later than he did and had volunteered to pick him up. Having her drive made it feel less like of a date for Sterling. It had been an outing of two friends, nothing more because he always, always drove on dates.

"This feels like old times," Alby said, pulling into his mom's driveway.

"How so?" he asked. "You've never driven me home before."

She gave him a look. "Many, many, *many* times I have driven you home."

"What? When?"

"Whenever you got too drunk at my house. Someone had to be responsible for y'all. Bunch of hooligans."

"I don't think that's right," he said.

"Just because you don't remember doesn't make it not true," she said.

"No, I believe you drove me home. What I don't believe is that I never kissed you in all that time. I remember me drunk. I thought I was Casanova."

"I never said you didn't try," she said.

"I did?"

She nodded. "A few times, three, I think."

"And you said no."

"That's right, I did."

"But you said yes to Hogue," he clarified.

"Hogue was sober," she said.

"And that's the only reason you chose him over me?" Sterling asked.

She stared thoughtfully at the house. "No, that's not the reason."

"Then why?"

"Because you were always larger than life to me. I saw you as more than the other boys, as better. The best, if I'm being honest. I didn't want anything that might tarnish that image, and I knew you didn't mean it. It was drunken confusion on your part, not an actual desire to kiss me."

"What if it had been an actual desire to kiss you?" he asked.

She faced him, resting her head thoughtfully on the back of the chair. "I still would have said no."

"Why?" he asked.

"Because you and me, we're not for each other," she said. "I've always known that, always understood, and never deluded myself otherwise, even when I deluded myself about other things."

He was vaguely frustrated by the statement, but he couldn't put his finger on the reason. "Why was I larger than life to you? Why did you see me as better?"

"Because you are," she said simply. Her index finger reached out and touched the dimple in his cheek, the one so well hidden under his stubble it was only recognizable to someone who knew it was there, someone who had known him forever and seen him smile often. Someone like Alby.

He faced his mom's house, reluctant to go in and end the evening. It had been a reprieve from the netherworld he now felt stuck in. He wasn't a kid, but neither was he a fully functioning adult.

"I need to get my own place again," he mused.

"I have my own place. It's not all it's cracked up to be."

"I was sorry about your parents." Her parents' death in a plane crash four years ago had been huge news. Sterling had attended the viewing, had even hugged her. Even so, he hadn't given Alby more than a cursory thought at the time, a sort of passing pity. But now he wondered how she had fared, all alone and suddenly thrust into the helm of her company.

"Thank you."

She stared through the top of the windshield, watching the stars while Sterling watched her. If someone had told him he would suddenly become curious about Alby Mowry, he would have laughed. But he was curious. What was she thinking as she made her silent inspection of the night sky? And why did he care? Was he that bored since Birdie went away that Alby was now high entertainment? Yes.

"I think you got cuter since we graduated," he blurted.

"Thanks, you too. I didn't think that was possible." Despite the words, her tone was bland.

"What's so interesting up there?" he asked.

"Meteor shower," she noted.

"Really?" he said, leaning forward. "Why didn't you say anything?"

"It's not the kind of information people usually find interesting.

Nature's not so cool, a lesson I learned one time when I pointed out a buck to Bess."

"Is that why she called you Bucky that year?" he asked.

"Yes."

"Ah." He had assumed it was because she had bucked teeth, but he had never looked closely enough to check. "I suppose I should go in before my cousin finds an excuse to come out. I think he has a crush on you."

"He's cute," Alby said, smiling vaguely.

What did that mean? "Are you purposely being mysterious?" he asked.

"What do you think?" she countered.

"I think I don't know you as well as I thought," he said.

"It's been ten years, Sterling. I don't think you know me at all," she said. She patted his knee. "Thanks for tonight, it was fun."

He slipped out of the car without responding, a perplexed frown on his face.

CHAPTER 10

"Tell me how this is supposed to help me," Alby commanded.

"Don't you trust me?" Sterling countered.

"Would you trust someone who told you to sit at a bar and hit on strangers?" Alby said.

"If I knew he had my best interest at heart and was going to be nearby watching." He settled his hands on her shoulders, bare shoulders because Alby was wearing a strapless dress. What was more, she had a nice figure when it wasn't being covered by old lady sweaters and khaki pants. It was like seeing a favorite little cousin after a long absence and realizing she had grown up, both disconcerting and endearing.

"You're not going to leave, really?" she asked, all big, soft eyes and an earnest, trusting expression.

"I'm not going to leave," he promised. He couldn't, wouldn't leave her; it would be like dropping a helpless puppy in the middle of the wilderness. "But you do need to practice the things we've been talking about, especially as it relates to men."

"Okay, I can do this. Put me in coach." She gave him a smile that was way too sweet to be seductive, and loveable for its attempt at bravery. She walked to the bar and took a seat. Sterling stood in the doorway, watching. Her shoulders were set and determined. She talked to the bartender who set a ginger ale and a bowl of pretzels before her. Her glance fell on the pretzels, nose wrinkled, and she spoke to the bartender again. He could imagine her saying something about the high instances of bacteria in communal pretzels because the bartender removed them. She opened her mouth to bite her thumbnail, remembered she had a manicure, and thought better of it.

A man entered the restaurant. It was a large space, the kind with a massive bar, dance floor, and seating area. Sterling watched him pause and hang his coat before turning to survey the space. He eyed Alby and one corner of his mouth turned up in a smile. Sterling tried to view her through the newcomer's eyes, but all he could see was her long, auburn hair and shapely backside, not the sweet, innocent set of her features, her easy smile or gentle expression. The man in question looked far too experienced and eager for a conquest, and for the first time Sterling began to have his doubts about the plan to get her some practice. She was vulnerable and inexperienced. What if she got hurt?

Someone sat on the stool next to Alby. She took a bracing breath and turned to face the newcomer, secretly hoping it wasn't a man. Of course it was, though. She could tell by the amount of space he took up and now, according to Sterling, she had to hit on him, to flirt with him, and get him to chat her up, maybe even to ask for her number.

When she could put it off no longer, she turned to face the newcomer with a smile that ended in flabbergasted surprise. "Sterling."

"Who?" he asked. "I don't believe we've met."

"You're right, sorry. You look like someone I know," Alby said.

"I get that a lot," Sterling replied. "What's a nice girl like you doing in a place like this?"

"Desperately trolling for male companionship," she replied. "How about you?"

"Same," he said, and she laughed. "What do you do? Or are you the independently wealthy sort who doesn't have to work, some kind of heiress."

"I'm a flight attendant," she said. "How about you?"

"I'm a pilot," he said.

"What's your favorite thing about being a pilot?"

"Knowing that at any given moment I have hundreds of lives in my hands," he said.

"These hands?" she asked, bringing them forward to grip them between both of hers.

"Be careful, I have pilot fingers," he said.

"Pilot fingers sounds like a disease from the eighteenth century," she said.

People were easing onto the dance floor. Sterling tugged her hands. "Wanna dance with me, stranger?"

"Let's," she said, allowing him to stand and lead her to the dance floor. He eased his arms around her, and they started to sway.

"I don't remember if we've ever danced together before," he said.

"Neither do I," she said.

"I thought women were supposed to remember things like that," he said.

"Only about men we have a romantic interest in," she said.

"How do you know you don't have a romantic interest in me if we just met?" he said.

"An excellent point, stranger," she said.

He spun her, expecting to catch her off guard, but she snapped back to him with the ease and resilience of an experienced dancer. "Where'd you get these dancing skills, ma'am?"

"Private lessons. I often go to the types of events that have dancing. My parents thought it was a good idea I learn."

"Excellent," he said, spinning her again. He was a better than average dancer. It was nice to be with someone who matched his skills.

"Good dancing must be in your genes," she said.

"How so?"

"Your cousin's a good dancer, too."

He narrowed his eyes at her. "You've danced with Taylor?"

"A time or two."

"What is with you two?"

"Why do you keep asking me that?" she said.

"Because you keep bringing him up."

"In context. Dancing with you reminds me of dancing with him," she said.

He frowned. "Shouldn't it be the other way around? You've known me longer, been my friend since kindergarten."

"No, actually. I've been your friend for a couple of weeks. I've been his friend for a few years. In fact, he and I have had many more heartfelt conversations than you and I have. Why does that make you scowl?"

"Because it does. Because it's wrong and weird to think of one of my friends getting on with my little cousin."

"Translation: even though I haven't wanted anything to do with Alby in all the years I've known her, I need to believe she hasn't defected from my adoring fan club in favor of my little cousin, with whom I feel in competition, even though he's lived in my too-big shadow for all of his life."

"I like you much better when you're saying nice things," he said.

"I'd like to believe your ego is big enough to survive hearing some truth now and again," she said.

"My ego resides in the trash heap now," he said.

"No, that's the problem; it doesn't. Your ego, or shall we say your pride, is so big that it keeps trying to get in your way. You somehow believe you should be immune to life's struggles, but Sterling, you're not. Life is hard sometimes, even for the likes of great big you."

It would have been a harder pill to swallow if it hadn't been said with so much sweetness. "The thing is, I was always supposed to be somebody bigger and better than what I am."

"Says who?" she asked.

"Says everybody. You know what it was like. Everyone had big hopes and dreams for me." He had been the king of this town once—team captain, homecoming and prom king, Mr. Popular, Mr. All America. Beloved by all, students and teachers alike.

"Who says you haven't fulfilled them?" she asked.

He quirked an eyebrow at her. "My girlfriend got pregnant by my best friend, my store is going under, I live with my mom, I'm practically penniless. I only have a job now because of your pity. I have never had a successful relationship, and now I have betrayal from my best friend and ex in that mix. Please tell me how my life looks like a success to you."

"Because, Sterling, the reason you are universally adored has never been about what you do but rather who you are. And that hasn't changed. You are smart and funny and kind and warm and strong, on the inside where it counts." She tapped his heart.

"How can you say that after the way I hurt you?"

"Because you did your best to make amends, and in all my life you're the only one who has."

He frowned, both pleased and disheartened by her words. "That's not right, Alby."

"It is what it is, Sterling," she said.

"Don't let it be. Stand up for yourself, find your fight."

She gave him another smile, an amused one this time. "What it must be like to see the world through your and Bess's eyes, if only for a day."

"You're going to in Atlanta."

She didn't reply, but she gave her head a little shake. He stopped dancing and gripped her biceps. "I'm serious here, Albertine. I will not stand by and watch you be a doormat in a new place. I can't stomach it. Pretend you're Bess, pretend you're me, or find your own voice, but you are not going to go into this weekend and get trampled. I will not allow it."

She stood on her toes and kissed his cheek. "You're very sweet, Sterling."

He blew out a breath. "I'm not actually, though, Alby. Ask anyone I've dated. They'll tell you that…"

She pressed her palm to his lips. "Learn to accept a compliment, old friend. And, I don't know, Sterling. It seems like if I'm turning over new leaves, you should be able to, too."

"I'll try," he promised, and was rewarded by another smile. He liked it when Alby smiled. It made him feel like all was right with the world again. Seeing her hurt or sad or distressed was…unsettling for reasons he couldn't articulate. Perhaps because she was a gentle soul who engendered his protectiveness.

"We're causing a traffic jam," he noted as they stood still while others swirled on the dance floor around them.

"A girl can only do so much on her own, Sterling. I'm waiting on a strong lead to guide me," Alby said.

"By all means, let me oblige you, Miss Mowry." He grasped her hand and flung her away from him, pulling her close again, smiling when she gave a bubble of laughter, pure and genuine. He'd been through a lot of pain and heartache since he grew up and had the stark realization life wasn't guaranteed to turn out okay. Not only did being with Alby feel like coming home, it felt a bit like an antidote. For the first time in a long time he felt like he could breathe freely again, like maybe someday he would get his life figured out. He had Alby to thank for that and it seemed to him he owed her more than he could currently repay, might ever be able to repay. *This weekend will not be like all the others,* he vowed. Alby would shine this weekend, if it was the last thing he ever did. And Heaven better help the next person who hurt or took advantage of her because if Sterling got to them first, there'd be nothing left.

CHAPTER 11

"*B*ess."

"Sterling, how did you get my number?"

"From Alby."

"Oh." She paused. "This is awkward, but I don't think I'm interested."

"Ease your mind because I'm definitely not," Sterling replied.

"Oh," she said, miffed now.

He chuckled. "I'm calling because I need a favor."

"You know me, Sterling. Always willing to help my fellow man."

"How about your fellow woman?" he asked.

"What?"

"Alby. She needs help."

"I'll say she does," Bess said. "Sorry, I don't know where that came from. I guess high school dies hard. What does Alby need and how could it possibly come from me?"

"Have you ever seen Alby in her professional capacity?" Sterling asked.

"No, but I can't imagine how it's different. Every time I picture Alby at work she's always carrying a tray of tea, trying to chat up the executives to make sure they're well fed and comfortable."

"That's not how it is. At all. She's like a different person. It's kind of nice, actually. For her, I mean. She's so…capable, so not sad."

"Wow."

"I know, it's sort of miraculous."

"No, I mean wow you. Sounds like someone has a crush on Alby."

Sterling laughed, hard. "You must be joking."

"I'm not. You should hear how you sound, all love struck."

"Bess, come on, it's Alby. It's just…You know we had that falling out at her house. I felt bad about it, really bad. And in trying to make it up to her, we sort of became friends, real friends. And then I saw her at work, and she's so different. It makes me realize how much more there is to her, more than we ever realized."

"If you say so. I still don't know what this has to do with me," she said.

"I've been trying to help her get ready for a business trip, but she needs a woman's touch, fashion advice, things like that. I thought you could help."

"Why me?" she asked.

"Because who else does she have? And it seems to me you kind of owe her."

She sighed expressively. "You're making some irritatingly good points tonight, Sterling. But how do I know she'll even want my help? Alby's always acted like a skittish kitten around me. She keeps a wary distance."

"She both wants and needs your help, and she'll take it, as long as you promise to be nice to her for the duration," he said.

"I'll try. It doesn't come naturally to me, especially not with her."

"Why not with her? What has it always been about with her? Why does she bug you so much?"

"Mostly because she lets me, but a little because of Hogue."

"What does Hogue have to do with it?" Did Bess know Hogue and Alby kissed in high school, and did she still hold it against them?

"Hogue puts up a good front making fun of her, but in private he throws her up to my face sometimes."

"How so?"

"As a paragon of womanhood, always mentioning how sweet and kind she is, how good she is at serving other people, those articles about her volunteer work. Little things that get under my skin. And the worst part is that he's not doing it on purpose. He honestly doesn't realize how he pits her against me, the dope."

Sterling smiled. "Sounds like true love."

She grunted.

"Right, new topic. Alby's expecting your call."

"I have to call her?"

"Do you really think Alby's going to call you and ask for anything? That's like telling a little kid to stick his hand in the viper's cage."

"Thank you so much for that," Bess said irritably.

"A sexy viper," Sterling amended.

"Why don't you call my husband and tell him that?"

"Believe me, he knows. He about yanked my arm out of socket when I kissed you," he said.

"Serves you right. That's what you get for kissing a halfway married woman," she said.

"And what did you get out of it?" he asked.

"The reminder that I'm still alive and that you're still a ridiculously good kisser, Sterling Thompson. And now as penance I have to give Alby a makeover."

"Twenty bucks says you'll have fun," Sterling said.

"It's going to take a lot more than that for me to have fun with Alby," Bess said.

Now two days later, she had never been more certain that it was a mistake to let Sterling talk her into helping Alby.

"How many outfits do you need?" Bess asked when they arrived at the upscale shopping complex an hour away from their home. Alby drove and it had been an awkward, stilted conversation on the drive. At the very least Bess was determined to enjoy it as a break from her kids. Her youngest was getting his molars, had been fussy, and hadn't let anyone in the house sleep. Now it was Hogue's turn to deal with it, and that made her smile.

"I don't know," Alby said.

Bess rolled her eyes. "Alby, come on. Do you know how many days you're going to be there or not?"

"Yes, I know how many days I'm going to be there, but I already have clothes. Surely I don't need a brand new outfit for every day I'm there."

Bess eyed her dowdy outfit. "Yes, you do."

Alby giggled, surprising her.

"What's funny?"

"Your expression, and the fact that you made zero attempt not to judge my clothes."

"You dress like you're ninety," Bess accused. "You always have."

"My parents were extremely conservative, and I'm the head of a corporation. Pardon me for not wanting to wear a thong to board meetings."

Bess put her hands over her ears. "Hearing Alby Mowry say 'thong' makes my ears bleed. Tell me how many days you're going to be there."

"Four days, three nights, and one of those is formal."

"A formal dinner for a business weekend?" Bess said.

Alby sighed. "Yes. They want me to buy their company. They're pulling out all the stops to make a good impression."

"If they want to impress you, then it really doesn't matter what you wear. They're going to suck up no matter what," Bess said.

"No, it doesn't work like that. These are Atlanta's elite. You know what they're like. They're going to be judging me every minute I'm there in every way."

"Oh," Bess said, understanding beginning to dawn. Even she would be uncomfortable in such a setting, and she was comfortable every-where. "All right, that gives me something to aim toward. What size are you?"

"Six, but I usually wear an eight because I don't like tight clothing."

"Yeah, you don't get a say anymore. From this moment on, you're nothing but a wallet to me."

"Is that what you said to Hogue on your wedding night?" Alby asked.

Bess looked at her, mouth ajar for a few seconds, and then she started to laugh. "I like this Alby. Let's keep her around today."

They entered the boutique of Bess's dreams, the sort of place she had never been able to afford. But Alby could, and there was a certain amount of fun to be gained vicariously. The clerk was the snooty sort who judged a customer's wardrobe by how much it cost. She easily dismissed Bess and even Alby who, until this point, had probably bought her clothes off the rack at Belk.

I'm going to enjoy this, Bess thought. Taking Alby's arm, she led her to the counter and deposited her with a flourish. "She needs the works, day outfits, night outfits, formalwear, shoes, and lingerie for a long weekend."

"Lingerie? No, Bess, I don't need…"

"Shh," Bess said, pressing her finger to her lips. "Wallets don't talk." The counter clerk, who had warmed considerably now, ushered Alby to a chair and retrieved fresh squeezed juice for her. Meanwhile she and Bess began arranging outfit after outfit, setting aside a pile for Alby to try on, which she did, dazed and overwhelmed. A few hours later, they were done, and Bess was pleased with the day's purchases.

"I'm never going to remember what to wear with which," Alby said.

"I know, I had her write a diagram for you," Bess said. "This was actually fun."

"Thanks for the vast amount of surprise in your tone. Feels good," Alby said.

Bess laughed, something she had been doing more than she would have imagined that day. "Do you want to grab lunch?"

"Absolutely. My treat."

"You don't have to," Bess said.

"Of course I do, you really helped me today. I would have gone to Belk," Alby said.

"Why? You're loaded. If I had your money, I'd probably fly to New York once a quarter for a wardrobe update."

"My parents started from humble beginnings, you know? They

never wanted people to think they were flaunting or being uppity. I guess they passed that on to me."

"That's weird," Bess said.

"I guess it wouldn't kill me to spend a tad more on my wardrobe," Alby said. "Today was sort of eye opening."

They went to a trendy café. Alby asked about mutual acquaintances and Bess's kids over lunch, both safe topics. It was Bess who veered off course.

"What's up with you and Sterling?"

"Nothing. We're friends," Alby said.

Bess squinted at her, searching for any telltale blushes or signs she was lying, but there were none. "Have you seen Sterling? He's gorgeous."

"You should see him without clothes on," Alby said, and Bess sputtered her coffee.

"What?"

Alby told her about her Friday laundry routine from high school, and Bess chuckled. "I always thought you were a loser for being the team's manager. Turns out you were just a perv."

"I prefer the term opportunist. It was the coach who made me do the laundry. Not my fault I was so forgettable none of them realized I was there," Alby said.

"You weren't forgettable to everyone," Bess said. When Alby didn't reply, she continued. "That was me, trying to goad you into confessing that you made out with my husband."

"He wasn't your husband then," Alby reminded her.

"He almost isn't again," Bess said. With a sigh, she pushed her coffee away.

"What happened there? I'll admit it was kind of a surprise when you and Hogue got together, but over the years it seemed to work somehow."

"I never wanted Hogue. I always wanted Sterling, but Sterling had his eyes on bigger things. I really thought he'd be married to a beauty queen by now."

"So did he, I think," Alby said.

Bess shrugged. "No matter what I tried, I could never get Sterling, not really. We flirted, we made out, he pulled away. It was a continuous cycle of frustration on my part. Hogue was always sort of there, always on standby, you know? That was how it started, I think. When I realized Sterling was really unavailable, I turned to my backup. I got pregnant, we got married, I felt trapped. And then somewhere along the way I fell in love with the big oaf. Every once in a while you get a glimpse behind the stupid and realize he's sweet and thoughtful and tender. Of course those times are few and far enough between to keep him aggravating, to keep you searching for them like specks of gold among the boulders of stupidity."

"Why the divorce?"

"Because it's hard, it's really, really hard, marriage and motherhood. Every day feels like a battle, and I'm tired. Hogue works long hours, and I feel like I'm in a marriage alone. I might as well be alone, hopefully there will be less fighting that way."

"I'm sorry. Is there anything I can do to help?" Alby asked.

"You really mean that don't you, Alby? You'd actually help us, if there was a way," Bess said, scrubbing at her eyes.

"Yes, I would do anything to help my friends. I thought you knew that about me."

"I do," Bess said, feeling sad and more than a little guilty. She got it now, what Sterling meant about Alby. There was more to her than they realized, more than the pathetic little hanger on of their youth. Maybe her parents' death had changed her in some way, maybe it was her job, maybe it was age and maturity. Or maybe it had been there all along and no one noticed. Either way, Alby was genuine, kind, deep, intriguing, and far funnier than Bess would have guessed. Or maybe Bess was the one who changed. In high school she hadn't realized how painful life could be, how much people like Alby made life easier and softened the journey. And since having her son, she now realized how much it hurt to be an outsider. Her son struggled with other kids. Bess couldn't help but feel like she was getting comeuppance for all the bullying she did in high school. No doubt about it, she hadn't been nice. It was that thought that compelled her to say the next thing.

"Let's get you a makeover."

By the time they arrived home, several hours later, Alby had been made over from head to toe, literally because she had also gotten a manicure and pedicure. She felt a bit like a dog that had been to the groomer's, but she was thankful for Bess's help, somehow understanding she had been given entrée into another world, Bess's world.

"Thanks for this, Bess. I really, really appreciate it."

Bess shrugged, looking uncharacteristically embarrassed. "It wasn't a big deal. You'll have to let me know how it goes."

"I'm not at all certain I can pull it off, even with the makeover," Alby admitted.

"You can, and if you get in trouble, channel me. Or call me, and I'll come handle them for you. I don't get to pull my claws out often enough now that I'm a mother," Bess said.

"I'll try hard to mimic you because I'm certain you could whoop them," Alby said. She waved and watched as Bess let herself into her house. Bess stood at the window and watched her drive away with an odd feeling of protectiveness that was unexpected but not necessarily unwelcome.

CHAPTER 12

*S*terling had been half hoping Alby would suggest riding to Atlanta together, but of course that wouldn't, couldn't happen. Not only would it not be appropriate to ride with his boss—he still wasn't used to that fact. Alby, *his boss*—but also Alby and her cousin, Peter, were going ahead of everyone else. That was perhaps the part she was most nervous about, those hours when she would be on her own with only her cousin as a companion. Sterling told her to text him, to keep him apprised of her progress.

I'm here. This room is FANCY. Chocolate-covered macadamias in the mini bar are more than twenty dollars.

You're a millionaire, he reminded her.

A millionaire with good sense. My lands, the inflation.

He chuckled at that, could picture the exact expression on her face as she sent the text. *Leave the room, Alby.*

Not sure if I can. Feet possibly glued to the floor.

Do some recon and report back. Right. Now. Albertine.

Aye-aye, sir.

He smiled and tucked his phone away, finishing what he needed to finish before he took off. Alby texted a couple of hours later and he realized he'd harbored a low-level anxiety waiting for it.

I found the Atlanta you.

He smiled. *How does he compare?*

Zero comparison. He is HOT!

I don't like that.

She sent him a winking emoji. *Found the Bess and Hogue and Stokes and Reams and Duncan. Haven't found me yet.*

He almost texted her that there was only one her, but he didn't because it felt too vulnerable.

In this world you and Bess are brother and sister, she continued.

Could have lived forever without that comparison, he said.

That's what Bess said.

She was also texting Bess? Interesting. As if thinking of her summoned her, his phone beeped with a text from Bess.

You need to get there.

Why? What's wrong?

First off, it's Alby. How long do you think she can hold off before she's refreshing everybody's drinks and basically making a doormat of herself? Second, I'm worried. The Atlanta you is Hart Wentworth.

The name was vaguely familiar, but Sterling couldn't place it. *So?*

Google, Bess replied, and he laughed. It was so like Bess to make him do the hard work himself instead of just telling him what he needed to know. He Googled the name, frowning as he scanned story after story on Hart Wentworth. *He'll destroy her,* he sent.

Get there, Bess directed. He didn't need to be told twice.

The drive to Atlanta had never felt longer, due in part to the horrendous traffic. Had it always been this bad and he'd forgotten, or was he feeling it more because he had a pressing drive to get there and rescue Alby? Maybe both things. All he knew was that he felt physically unable to stop drumming his fingers on the steering wheel or flicking the radio. He'd texted Alby twice since her last missive and hadn't heard a thing. Was that good or bad? He had no idea.

He arrived, tossed his keys to the valet, and hustled inside. Once there, however, he paused, straightened his clothes, and looked for a good vantage point. In football it was impossible to plan a good attack without strategizing and studying the enemy. That was why his old coach had made them watch all those old game films, to study the opponent, to find their weaknesses as well as their strengths. It was a lesson Sterling had taken to heart, and he never did anything without a little preparation. Reading about Hart Wentworth made him understand that he had vastly underestimated the situation. Not only that, but he'd sent Alby in blind, had essentially shoved her into a knife fight weaponless.

Hart Wentworth and his sister, Whitney, were like royalty of old. They had the title and prestige but were lacking money. Their company was an old and storied one with an excellent reputation. Unfortunately for them, reputation hadn't been enough to sustain them through the last economic setback. They were close to going under. They needed Alby and her money, desperately needed her to invest in their floundering company or risk losing it forever. They would be willing to do whatever necessary to secure it, up to an including seduction and possibly marriage. The merger of the two companies had the potential to be a billion dollar enhancement. With that kind of money on the line, all bets were off. And now Alby, sweet, gentle Alby, was caught in the crosshairs. They would eat her alive, and it was up to him, Sterling, to save her. Also by any means necessary.

It was cocktail hour. Sterling found a spot behind the curtain and watched. Whitney Wentworth was definitely the Bess in this scenario, though, he thought fondly, Bess could likely take her and come out on top. Not only was Bess prettier, but she was craftier and more cutthroat. Whitney kept shooting looks to her brother, as if for direction. In their town, Bess called the plays on her own.

Hart was clearly the forerunner and the center of everything. He stood at the edge of the room, talking, laughing, and flirting with some woman. At least he hadn't gotten to Alby yet. And this woman looked more his type, her long auburn hair arranged in some kind of... Sterling tipped his head at her, taking stock of the way the sophisticated cocktail dress molded to her shapely body. He pulled out his phone and fired off an outraged text to Bess.

WHAT DID YOU DO TO ALBY??

He could almost hear Bess laughing at him when she replied. *Didn't realize she had all that hiding there, did you? Me neither. Should have done this to her years ago. How's she holding up to Hart?*

Don't know yet. Haven't made contact. Thinking of the best way to play it. So far it looks good, but...

But she's far more innocent than he is, and if he gets close enough he'll destroy her? Bess guessed.

Yes. But she's my boss.

She was our Alby first.

Sterling tucked his phone back in his pocket, pondering that. She was his friend and responsibility, more so since he'd trampled her feelings and insulted her. Alby had spent her life in their small town, insulated from the world. She likely had no idea what a man like Hart Wentworth was capable of, nor all the ways he would be willing to use her to get what he wanted. She was in big trouble, and it was up to Sterling to protect her. Whether she liked it or not. With that thought in mind, he straightened his tie and strode forward.

Alby caught sight of him in her peripheral and turned to him with a smile of...what was that? Amusement? Conspiracy? He smiled in return, though his was full of warning. Her smile faltered, lashes fluttering. She opened her mouth to speak, but he preempted her.

"Sorry I'm late, sweetheart. Traffic was a nightmare." He eased his arm around her, leaned forward and kissed her cheek, cinching her close to him as he faced the other man. "Who's your friend?"

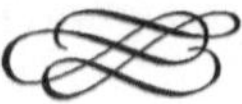

$\mathcal{A}$lby stared at him, blinking in silence, which was fine because it gave him and Hart a chance to size each other up. Hart wore a well-cut suit that likely cost more than Sterling's car. He clearly came from old money, but Sterling had the feeling he was untested. He likely played polo and rode horses. Sterling had waged war with mental illness, his father's and his own. And so far he was on top. In his mind, that made him the stronger man.

"Hart Wentworth," he said, extending his hand.

Sterling let go of Alby to shake it. "Sterling Thompson."

"Sterling?" Alby said, still blinking at him.

"Yes?" he replied, giving her his most megawatt smile. He glanced at her empty hands, his smile slipping to a frown. "Sweetheart, neither of us has a drink yet. What do you say you accompany me to the bar? So nice to meet you, Mr. Wentworth. I'm certain we'll get a chance to interact more later." Not waiting for a response, he took Alby's hand and led her behind him to the bar, not pausing until they reached it.

"What was that?" she hissed.

"I didn't know you were meeting with Hart Wentworth this week-end," he whispered.

"So? What difference does that make?"

"So do you know who he is, what his reputation is?" he returned.

"Yes. I did a lot of background on both him and his company. He's a rounder, a notorious playboy."

"And did it occur to you that he would try to make you his next conquest?"

"Yes." She reached for her soda, giving the bartender a polite smile.

"That's an awfully casual attitude," he said, miffed for reasons he didn't understand. She knew he was going to hit on her? Was willing to let it happen?

"Just because a man hits on me doesn't mean I'll accept. It does happen occasionally, believe it or not. But I have standards. I'm not desperate." Two little spots of color appeared in her cheeks.

Uh-oh. Warning. Danger. Part of him wanted to keep pushing her. He had never seen Alby in a temper before. What would that be like? The other part of him realized the moment was too critical for games. "I know that, Alby. No one looking at you right now would ever believe you're desperate but you are..." he trailed off, not wanting to insult her or hurt her feelings.

"What?" she asked, staring up at him in defiance which, perversely, made him want to smile.

"You're innocent."

Her frown deepened.

"Aren't you?" he said, his tone softer and gentler now. "Unless you're hiding some past as a femme fatale I don't know about, you don't have a lot of experience fielding men like Hart. They're used to getting what they want, will use anyone standing in their way. I thought if I took you out of the running, it might be the best way to protect you, to give you a chance to objectively look at his company without being pursued, without being in danger."

She studied him in consternation, swirling the ice in her soda without sipping it. "I'm not certain I'm not angry with you."

He couldn't resist smiling a little. "I'm not certain I don't want you to be."

She looked away, blushing faintly. She took a breath, held it, and let it out slowly. "You think I'm naïve, but I'm not certain you under-stand all the ways you've now complicated our lives."

"Tell me," he said, reaching for some pretzels from the communal bowl. Normally he didn't partake in such a germ fest, but he had skipped lunch, and he was starving.

"Word of this alleged relationship between us won't stay between you and me and Hart Wentworth. It's going to spread through my company, to your fellow managers, my employees, of which you are one." She took a tentative sip of the soda.

"That's a bit awkward," he agreed. "But." He set down his drink and placed both hands on her shoulders. "You and I have a long history together, and we're from a very small town. It's not altogether impos-sible that you'd end up with someone you've known forever, someone who works for you. And, I must point out again: it's your company. You can do whatever you want."

"I wasn't thinking of me, Sterling. I was thinking of you. People are going to talk about you, about the reasons you're allegedly with me. You ready for that? You ready to be labeled a gold digger?"

He flinched, his fingers tightening reflexively on her shoulders. "People have said worse about me. Besides, we know the truth."

"That we're not actually together," she affirmed. She gave a little giggle and pressed her lips together, trying to push it back.

"What?" he asked, his thumbs making little circles on her shoul-ders. Apparently keeping herself under cover for nearly three decades had preserved the creamy expanse of her because her skin was flaw-less and smooth, and that was possibly the oddest thing he'd ever noticed about a woman.

"This is like a book I read where the woman pretended to be the man's date for a weekend. It was preposterous, and yet now I'm living it."

"It could be kind of fun," he said.

"It could be kind of awkward," she countered.

"How so?" he asked.

"Because at some point it's likely going to encompass more than slipping your arm around me and inferring we're together," she said.

"What do you think it's going to entail?" he asked. He eased slightly closer and leaned in to whisper. "Do you think maybe we're going to have to kiss?"

She perched on her toes and touched her hand to his chest for balance as she reached his ear. "It means we have adjoining rooms."

"What?" he exclaimed. "How did that happen?"

"I did it. I thought it would be a handy way to reconnoiter at the end of the day. I thought I'd need the moral support. And now it just looks immoral."

He snorted a laugh.

"It's not funny," she said, though she was smiling.

"It is very funny, and also convenient." He wagged his eyebrows.

"Sterling," she said. "You should not be enjoying this so much."

"I definitely should, and so should you. I mean, come on, Alby. You're supposed to be showing the world something different here. You and me having a fling is definitely different."

"Yes, but is it believable?" she said.

He looked at her, thinking. The women he'd dated had all been broken in some way, badly damaged and desperate for a fix. Sterling was a fixer by nature. It had seemed natural that he always be the one attempting a heroic rescue in some way. But Alby wasn't broken. Maybe she was frayed a bit by loneliness and rejection, but her heart was whole and pure, filled with goodness and love. All in all, she was way too good for him.

"We'll have to make it so," he said, bringing her fingers to his lips and kissing them. Far from looking pleased, Alby regarded him warily.

"I think there's something you haven't thought of," she said.

"What's that?"

"In trying to protect me from him, you may end up doing more damage yourself. I'm not used to this." She pointed between them. "Attention, effort, wooing. What if you turn my head, Sterling Thompson?"

"What if I do?" he asked.

"I'm not the kind of woman who can go from man to man. When I fall, I'm going to do it hard, and it will only be once," she warned.

"Then don't fall for me, Alby. Too much risk, and I'm not worth it," he said seriously. He kissed her fingers again and let them go. "This, all of this that's about to happen between us, is for pretend. Don't forget."

"Don't let me."

"Yes, Ma'am," he agreed, tossing her a wink. "Now, are you ready to go and face the music I've created?"

"One more thing." She tugged his lapels. "How does this end? Which one of us will be the bad guy?"

"Neither. It'll fizzle, and we'll remain friends."

"Why will it fizzle?"

"Because you insisted on eating peaches, and I couldn't take it," he said, earning a laugh from her. His hands settled at her waist.

"Don't ask me to give up peaches for you, Sterling. I cannot. I *will* not."

"You're breaking my heart, Albertine."

"Don't return the favor, Sterling." She kissed her finger and touched it to his dimple.

"Alby?"

Alby's cousin, Peter, stood beside them. His tone was loaded both with questions and disapproval. Sterling and Alby tensed as they faced him. For Sterling, the man was an unknown quantity. He hadn't grown up local, had apparently only signed on to the company in the intervening years since high school. Right away that made him an object of suspicion. He was only a couple of years older than Alby, but his attitude was pedantic at least, proprietary at best.

"Hello, Peter. You remember Sterling?"

"Our new project manager? Yes, I remember Sterling," Peter said, his eyes flicking to Sterling with undisguised suspicion. "I wasn't aware you two were so…close?"

"We go all the way back to kindergarten," Sterling said. He took Alby's hand and gave it a squeeze. "Remember Mrs. Albright? That leg brace she wore scared the wits out of me."

"She was all right," Alby said, returning the gentle pressure of his hand.

"She liked girls better than boys," Sterling said.

"What teacher wouldn't? Y'all were heathens. Still are," she said.

"Not me. I've reformed, Miss Mowry," Sterling replied. He tossed her another smile and turned back to Peter. "Excuse us, please. I've kept Alby away for too long, I think." He skirted by Peter, tugging Alby behind him. When they were a safe distance away, he brought her beside him and whispered. "Do you trust that guy?"

"He's family," Alby replied.

"But do you trust him?"

Alby turned to glance at Peter who was still watching them, eyes narrowed. "I don't know. We weren't close growing up. I've only gotten to know him in the last few years and I...I just don't know, Sterling."

"Unless or until you do, don't let down your guard around him. I'm going to keep him in my scopes this weekend until we get it figured out."

"Five minutes into this fake relationship and you're already speaking of us as a unit. Guess that means I'm a bit behind in my nagging," she said.

He tried and failed to imagine her nagging. Alby was the sort who would either do it herself or lead by example. That would be a blessed relief after some of the women he'd dated who had played games, been passive-aggressive, or downright aggressive. What would it be like to be with someone like Alby, someone healthy and whole? Someone who had her life together? Sterling couldn't fathom.

"I think you'll find, as time goes on, there are many things we're behind on," he said, quirking an eyebrow as his glance fell to her lips.

Predictably, Alby blushed. Unpredictably, she replied, "Well, Sterling, I have always prided myself on being a fast learner."

"Wow, Alby, wow," he had time to say before they were sucked into the vortex of social interaction.

CHAPTER 14

Seemingly everyone wanted a piece of Alby. It was highly entertaining for Sterling who knew her both ways, as sweet Alby of old and the accomplished CEO of a massive company, Albertine Mowry. As he scanned the room, he realized he was the only person in possession of the former knowledge, the only one who knew Alby's secret—that she was not, in fact, always the confident heiress and boss she seemed. That she had been something of an outcast for as long as he could remember. Looking at her now, no one could guess. Bess had done a number on her outward appearance. The hair, makeup, and dress were on point. Even her shoes looked classy and expensive, and he knew nothing about women's shoes.

As they circulated around the room, she was warm and friendly and polite, lobbing gentle, informed questions at everyone they encountered. She introduced Sterling as "my friend," and he wholeheartedly approved. This wasn't the type of scenario where you flaunted a relationship; it was the kind where you left people guessing. Though, as they wandered from place to place hand in hand, there was little left to question.

"You are very good at this," he murmured in her ear after one such conversation.

"Holding hands?" she guessed, looking at their linked fingers. "I'm a natural."

"Schmoozing with strangers," he whispered. She remembered names and pertinent facts with aplomb.

"I like people, and I especially like to make people feel good. My dad always said the person in front of you should feel like the most special and important person in the world. Because they are."

"Wise words from a good man," he said.

"Yes." She sighed. "I miss him so much, Sterling. My mom, too. They were gone too soon and too sudden."

"I know, Alby, and I'm sorry," he said, easing his arm around her and giving her a squeeze. She rested her head on his shoulder a beat before they were interrupted again.

"I cannot believe I haven't had a chance to say hi to y'all before now." Whitney Wentworth stood before them, her dazzling smile not quite meeting her eyes. Her gaze eased from Alby to Sterling and settled. Over her shoulder, he saw her brother, Hart, watching them and pretending not to. Obviously the sister had been sent in as a distraction, to try and pry Sterling away from Alby.

"Hello, Whitney. Such a lovely gathering. Your gown is gorgeous," Alby said.

Whitney blinked at her, probably trying to sift the words for hidden meanness. *There is none,* Sterling wanted to tell her. *She means every word. She's as kind and genuine as she seems.* "Thank you," Whitney said. "And I just love your dress." It was also clear, at least to Sterling, that Whitney was trying and failing to find a way to insult Alby's dress. There wasn't a way, however, because the dress was perfect, and it fit her like a glove. *Well done, Bess,* he thought. It hurt his heart to know this woman had her teeth out, intending to use them on Alby. When she set her sights on him, there was not one flicker of temptation in response.

"And who do we have here?" she asked with all the ease of someone who was used to bending men to her will and whims.

"Sterling Thompson," he said. "Alby's boyfriend."

Alby gave a small flinch. They hadn't lied so blatantly before, but subtlety would not work on the likes of Whitney Wentworth.

"Oh, how nice," she said insincerely. "How long y'all been together?"

Sterling and Alby looked at each other. "We go back since kindergarten, but we didn't get together until recently," Sterling said.

"What brought that on?" Whitney asked. "I sense a story."

"It was one of those things. I was in the market for a new job."

"Oh?" Whitney's eyebrows rose, her interest notching. "And what do you do now?"

Sterling smiled. "Project manager. For Alby." He turned to her and squeezed the back of her neck.

She jerked away from him and held out her hand. "Stop that, now. You know I'm ticklish. It's undignified."

He hadn't known she was ticklish, of course. But now that he did… She shook her head at him, as if reading his mind. The temptation was strong to do it again, but he refrained. She was right—this was a dignified affair. Later, though, he'd come back to it.

"Look at y'all. Lost in your own little interlude," Whitney said, her tone soured by more than a little bitterness.

"Y'all hogging our guest of honor, Whit?" Hart asked as he casually inserted himself into their group. He draped his arm on Whitney's shoulders. She slipped her arm around his waist in the same casual manner.

"We've been discussing Alby and Sterling's romance," Whitney said.

"Have you, now? What did I miss?" Hart said.

"Did you know that Sterling is a project manager in Alby's company?" Whitney asked, her tone stuffed with amusement.

"Really? Now that's tricky. How y'all navigate that?" Hart asked with seemingly genuine interest.

"We go back a ways," Sterling said.

"And Sterling's always been good about taking direction, so long as he respects the person giving the orders," Alby said. "He's mature and reasonable, not competitive and misogynistic."

"Well, thank you for that," Sterling said, giving her hand a squeeze.

"Aren't you two just the cutest?" Hart said. "Does your maturity extend to allowing y'all to dance with someone else? Because I think it's time we set the standard here." He gestured to the empty dance floor.

"Absolutely," Alby said, letting go of Sterling to extend her hand to Hart.

"I guess that leaves us," Whitney said, smiling up at Sterling.

"Would you like to dance, Miss Wentworth?"

"Such manners, Mr. Thompson," she said, bestowing her hand daintily in his like the belle she was. Their towns weren't far apart in distance, but Atlanta was a whole other universe. Currently they were at a resort in Buckhead, driving the point home further. Here people still observed the rules of old society with debutante balls, customs and rules that had otherwise become obsolete. Sterling knew enough to understand that he would never fit in this world, but neither did he want to. It comforted him to know that Alby was much closer to his way of thinking than theirs. She had never been a deb and, while she may have attended a few more formal parties than he had, they weren't her scene, either.

"I don't see you and Alby together," Whitney wasted no time in saying.

"You don't know either one of us," Sterling pointed out.

"I've known *of* Alby for years, of course. We've always circled the same drain. You're something new and different, but I know the type."

"And what is that?" he couldn't help asking.

"Charming and beloved, a golden boy."

That may have been true at one point. He saw no need to point out to her how much the status quo had changed. "And how do you not think that fits with Alby?"

"She's very sweet."

"She is, but you've clearly never seen her in action. I wouldn't underestimate her."

That brought a frown. He wondered if they thought they could bring Alby here and manage her, convince her to buy into their company with little fuss and fanfare. For Alby's sake, he wanted to make sure that didn't happen. Maybe she would decide to invest, but it would be hard-won after much wooing and proof of revenue and worth.

"You must have some in with her," Whitney cooed.

He shook his head. "Alby does what Alby will. It's her company. I have neither input nor sway, nor do I want it. You see, Miss Wentworth, I am lacking business ambition completely."

"Then why do you work in business, Mr. Thompson?"

That gave him pause. He had jumped at the job at Alby's company in desperation. It had seemed like a lifeline, and it was. But was it what he actually wanted to do? For the last few years his bookstore had started to feel like one more albatross, weighing him down. But now that he was away from it, he longed to go back. "An excellent question."

"At the very least you must have some insight into how she's leaning where we're concerned."

"On the contrary, I have no idea. But I have to tell you that even if I did, I wouldn't tell you. My first and only loyalty is to Alby, not a stranger I just met."

"She's very lucky to have you," Whitney said, as if he deserved some kind of commendation for being loyal to his supposed girlfriend.

"If you really knew us, you'd say it's the other way around," he said and meant it. Alby was everything good and kind and pure about the world. He was...not.

"Looks like my brother might want to give you a run for your money," Whitney commented, her gaze fastened on Alby and Hart as they danced merrily together, talking and laughing like old friends. Sterling neither liked nor trusted the ease he saw between them. But of course he couldn't let Whitney know that. She was looking for any cracks between him and Alby; it was up to him not to let her see any.

"He clearly doesn't know Alby. Loyalty is what's most important to her," Sterling said and realized it was true.

"She's a paragon of perfection, isn't she?" Whitney said. Her snide tone was an invitation to pile on, to make fun of Alby. It was a tone he'd heard all his life in regard to Alby. Somehow her softness made her a target for everyone unhappy with the state of their own life. It had always irritated Sterling, how easily she became a target for bullies. But now the feeling went beyond irritation. He glanced at Alby. No more. As long as he had breath, no one would ever trample Alby again.

"I think so," he said sincerely.

Whitney blinked at him, taken aback by his earnestness. "I guess you've both met your match."

"Time will tell," he said mildly. The song ended and he went to retrieve Alby. "My turn, I think." He extended his hand to her.

"We'll talk more later," Hart said, handing her over.

Alby nodded and smiled. She and Sterling danced in silence a minute. Having her tucked safely and cozily in his embrace felt reassuring and secure. There was a comforting familiarity with Alby he hadn't experienced with other women, and he liked it. He didn't have to pretend with her, to try and be perfect. She had seen him at his worst and liked him anyway. There was a blissful sort of freedom in that. "What were you two talking about?" he asked.

"This and that. Hart is funny. He was telling me stories about people I don't know, asking why he'd never seen me at any polo or horse events."

"Why hasn't he? You could've gone that route."

"Can you see me as a deb? My lands." She shook her head.

"Yes, actually. You have all the social graces, the money, the looks. The only thing you're lacking is a smug sense of superiority."

"I'll work on that. What were you and Whitney talking about?"

"You, mostly. She was trying to feel me out about you, about us, about your interest in their company."

"What did you tell her?"

"That you are way out of my league and I have no idea what your company plans are."

"Sterling, don't be crazy. I think it's clear what our company plans are, if you've been paying close attention," she said.

He leaned in and bit her neck, causing her to squeal and jump. He followed it up with a squeeze and a kiss on the cheek. "All joking aside, Alby, you look amazing tonight," he added.

"Thank you. You look fairly dashing yourself. I always love it when you dress up."

He raised his eyebrows. "When have you seen me dressed up?"

"Sports banquets, homecoming, prom, the like. And then there was that picture of you from that triathlon you did a few years back." She used her right hand to fan her face. "Have mercy, Sterling."

"Now when did you see a picture of that?"

"I ran into your mom at the market, and she showed me your picture," she said.

"You talked to my mom?"

"I've talked to your mom on many, many occasions. Though I have to say I think she had the wrong impression about how close we were. She always updated me on you and said things like, 'But of course he's probably already told you this himself.' I never had the heart to correct her, mostly because it's how I wished it was, that we'd been the kind of friends who stayed in contact."

"To be fair, I didn't stay in contact with anyone besides Duncan," he said.

"Why not?"

"Because I wanted to run away and never come back, to gain some distance between myself and high school," he said.

"But why? Why do you hate home so much? You come from good people, you had good friends. What's not to love?"

He blew out a breath. How to explain it to her when it was so hard to articulate in his own mind? "I always wanted more than what I had. I wanted to be bigger, better. It's why I went to college and made other friends. But when I was with them…It was just being me in a different place."

"What's wrong with being you, Sterling? You've always been wonderful."

"Alby," he said, shaking his head.

"What?"

"I wish I had your talent for always seeing the best in people, myself included. I look at our town and I see a bunch of local yokels, ignorant people who've never gone farther than ten miles from home. I look at me and I see a washed up has been with no sense of direction, no ambition, and nothing to show for my life."

"I look at our town and I see a community, people who support each other when times are hard. Not perfect people, by any means, but people who are willing to overlook our imperfections. And I look at you, and I see," she paused and eased closer, slipping her arms around his neck, "I see so much potential, Sterling. You could be anything."

"But what? I have no idea what I should be."

"Let's figure it out," she said. She squeezed the back of his neck. "You have so many amazing gifts, Sterling, so much to offer. The trick is figuring out how to use it. When we put our minds together, I know we can come up with something."

When she said it, he almost believed her. Maybe it was that simple, having someone who had known him forever helping him sort his strengths from his weaknesses and find some direction. He began to have hope it might be possible.

"Hey, Alby." His grip tightened on her waist.

"Yes?"

What was he going to say? He had no idea, and he was saved from figuring it out when the announcement for supper was made.

CHAPTER 15

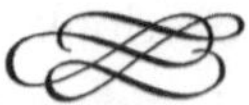

Atlanta was a strange and mystifying place. In her own little corner of the world, Alby was familiar with the dichotomous nature of her life. In the past there had been two Albys. The first was Home Alby, beloved only daughter of the town's wealthiest business owners. Her father had trained her to take over the business from an early age, including her on business trips and explaining exactly how everything worked. Her mother had worked to teach her other things —kindness, hard work, good manners, ladylike behavior, modesty, humility. She would be eternally grateful for all their hard work on her behalf. Sometimes she wondered if they'd harbored a prescient understanding that their lives would be cut short, that she'd need to learn to survive without them. Whether that was true or not, she had felt as prepared as she could be to assume her father's mantel and become the twenty four year old CEO of his company. Thanks to his gradual introduction, others had been okay with it, too. Alby was a familiar face around the company, long before she took it over.

In addition to being Home Alby, she had been School Alby— unpopular tagalong who didn't seem to fit anywhere. Sometimes the reality of her station in life had bothered her, but not deeply, not at her core because she'd always had her parents, always known who she was and that she was loved by them regardless. Plus school had been temporary, or so she thought.

And then, after school ended and after her parents were gone, she became Work Alby, the woman in charge of seemingly everything. What's more, she *liked* being in charge, thrived on the day to day running of a massive corporation.

And then Sterling Thompson came around and threw everything into chaos.

She had planned the party to reunite the old gang. She wasn't so deluded that she had attempted to stay in contact with anyone from their group. But it had been ten years and their reunion was coming up. A get together beforehand seemed in order, and it was the perfect way to celebrate being ten years out of school. Or so she thought. In reality it had been one more highlight of how much she would never fit in. Worse, she'd heard Sterling say it in his own words. That had been akin to getting maimed by a beloved pet. While she hadn't harbored any sort of crush on him, Sterling had always been larger than life to her, sort of like a big brother who was her age. He had been like King Midas back in the day; everything he touched turned to gold. Everyone had adored him, Alby included. And he had been *nice.* She had never once heard him make fun of her behind her back the way the other kids did. On the contrary, she had occasionally heard him step in and tell them to knock it off.

After hearing him say such awful, hurtful things about her, she vowed to stay away from him, so sure she would never be able to forgive and forget the awful night. But, being Sterling, he had charmed her into doing so. Not only that, but they had become friends, real friends, for the first time in their lives. No longer was she tagalong little Alby, the sports manager to his team captain. They were equals now. Well, not really. Technically she was his boss and he was her employee. But Alby didn't like to think of things in those terms. To her he was and would always be Sterling, the ridiculously handsome boy beloved by all, the prince in every fairytale.

Only now everything was topsy turvy and it might all be Sterling's fault. Alby still wasn't clear on that part. One minute she had been flirting—actually flirting—with Hart Wentworth, and the next she was pretending to be Sterling's girlfriend with seemingly no in between. And now it was supper. Sterling sat at the head table along with her, Hart, Whitney, Peter, and Peter's wife, Gloria. The other project managers sat at another table, the table where Sterling was originally supposed to be. They darted glances between her and Sterling then bowed their heads, whispering. Peter was staring daggers at her, too. Whitney and Hart kept sending each other covert looks. And then there was Sterling who, in between courses, rested his arm on the back of her chair, his fingers skimming distractedly along her shoulder. That more than anything was causing her brain to skitter. She had always been alarmingly responsive to touch. Now that her parents were gone, she received far too little of it. What was she going to do, hug Peter? She almost laughed at that. She'd have better luck hugging a cactus, and with better results, too.

Sterling must have caught her smile because he raised his eyebrows at her in question. She gave him a little shake of her head. There was no possible way to explain her wild tangle of thoughts. She felt she had done an admirable job of staying present during the meal, of parrying Hart's probing and Whitney's subtle jabs, Peter's condescension, and Gloria's shrill observations. But now she was starting to become tired and her mind was spinning off in other directions.

"Well, this has been a delightful evening, y'all." This came from Sterling who had been unnaturally quiet and subdued through the evening, content to let Alby take the lead in conversation. It was surprising, to say the least. Sterling was usually the center of things, or he had been, back in the day, the unmitigated leader of their group. Even Bess had looked to him for direction, had practically said, "how high" when he said, "jump." He rested his hand on her bare knee, and Alby resisted the urge to jump herself. If only she wasn't so ridiculously ticklish. It was something about herself she'd always hated. "But I think my girl is growing sleepy. If y'all will excuse us, I'm going to take her upstairs and put her to bed."

Alby was fairly certain her cheeks were glowing. Did people think he meant something naughty by that? Had he intentionally meant for it to sound that way? Regardless, it was now her turn to speak. "Sterling's right. This evening has been lovely. Thank you all so much. I'm looking forward to tomorrow. Rest well, y'all." Their goodbyes were polite, but their eyes were on her as Sterling stood, pulled back her chair, and took her hand to help her up. He kept it as they headed toward the elevator.

She waited until the doors were closed to let go, lean against the wall, and close her eyes. "Doing all right?" he asked.

She nodded, but she wasn't certain she meant it. Was she mad at him? She couldn't say for certain. The way he'd inserted himself into the weekend without consulting her rankled her, but was it worth a fight when his intentions had been good? She wasn't sure. What she did know was that she was tired. Exhausted, really.

"Thanks for getting me out of there." One thing she knew for certain, if he hadn't intervened, she would still be there, might be stuck there for several more hours. Alby was good at the social graces until it came to goodnight. She never knew how to make a polite exit. She wasn't sure the exit tonight had been graceful, but at least it had been speedy.

"You're welcome. You looked like you were beginning to zone," Sterling said.

"I was. It's harder than I thought, playing a part, being on guard all the time." It had been exhausting to try and keep an eye out for Hart's flirtation, Whitney's digs, and Peter's suspicion. Her eyes landed on Sterling in surprise. "Having you there helped a lot. Thank you, Sterling." He had parried everyone gracefully, making himself the first line of defense for anyone attempting to wound her. He was especially adept at intercepting Whitney's little potshots. And he had done it so artlessly she hadn't realized until now.

"You're welcome, Albertine," he said softly, giving her a slow smile.

She faced the button, urging the elevator to go faster. Sterling had never called her Albertine before they became friends the last few weeks. Other kids had used it as a way to torment her, to remind her how different she was, how much she would never fit in or be like them. Sterling had never done that to her. And the way he said it now still wasn't a taunt. It was more like…a caress? Or maybe that was merely the way it made her feel to hear it, as if he'd slid his fingers along her face in the gentlest possible manner. She closed her eyes and shook her head to clear it. This was Sterling. Of course he didn't mean it like that. He was no doubt teasing her in some way she had yet to discern, a sisterly way, perhaps. She had no experience with men, save for a few unsuccessful dates. The friendship she had with his cousin, Taylor, was the closest she had to a real friendship with any man, save Sterling. Unless she counted her driver, Paulo. And people you paid couldn't actually be counted as friends because, well, they were being paid. Of course they had to be nice.

You're paying Sterling, a hateful little voice reminded her. With effort, she shook it off. *Sterling and I go back farther than my payments.* Besides, Sterling wasn't in it for the career advancement. She knew enough about him to believe that. He had never been avaricious or career ambitious. He had always only ever wanted to be a hero.

She opened her eyes wide, and tapped his chest. "I've got it."

"What?" he asked.

"Your future," she said. She had some ideas about his career direction, all of a sudden.

The elevator dinged on their floor. He waited until they stepped out to grin at her. "Yeah? Do tell, Alby." He trailed behind her to her room and waited while she pulled out her key. She thought they would have the discussion there in the doorway; she was wrong. He followed her inside, took off his shoes by the doorway, and shrugged out of his jacket and tie, draping them on the chair. After that, his gaze traveled the room appreciatively. "Swanky. I haven't glimpsed my room yet, but something tells me it's not like this."

Alby felt unaccountably embarrassed over that. "Your room is smaller. This is the presidential suite. Yours is the assistant suite. But we can trade, if you want. I'm not overly fussy about things like that." She sank into the plush couch and slipped off her shoes with a satisfied sigh.

Sterling was smirking at her now. He walked to her bed and plopped across it. "We are not trading rooms, you crazy girl. You're the president of the company. Enjoy the perks that come along with it."

She rolled her eyes, too tired to respond. Sterling patted the space beside him on the bed. "I've got to get out of this dress first."

He sat up on one elbow. "If you insist, Alby, but if anyone asks, I put up a fight."

"Ugh," she muttered, too tired for his charm. She reached for the zip on her dress but couldn't quite grasp it. "Do you mind?" She turned her back to him, intending for him to get it started so she could take over, but he unzipped it all the way, his fingers skimming along her spine. She kept her back to him, hoping he wouldn't notice the flush of her cheeks. It was just Sterling, but he was still a man.

"There you go, Miss Mowry," he said silkily.

"Back in a jiff," she said, ducking into the bathroom, clothes in hand. She emerged a minute later in yoga pants and a hoodie. Sterling studied her, perplexed. "What?"

"I've never seen you dressed like that, so casual."

She blew out a breath and crawled onto the space beside him, yawning as she stretched out. When the yawn was over, she spoke. "My parents were pretty adamant that I dress befittingly. They weren't so much into casual attire. It's only since they've been gone that I've fully embraced leisurewear."

"Hmm. It's cute," he said. He tapped the hair piled atop her head. "This coming down, too?"

"Later. Too tired." Her face was half mashed to the mattress, muffling her words. Her eyes opened wide when Sterling leaned over and began plucking the pins out of her hair. When he was finished, he ran his fingers through it, loosening it gently.

"You were telling me about my future, gypsy woman," he whispered.

"This," she said, eyes going closed again, lips still mashed into the mattress. "Scalp massager. Will pay you lots. All my monies, take it."

"Baby, I will do it for free. I love to play with a woman's hair."

Alby snorted a laugh and pressed her lips together.

"What, you think that makes me odd?" he asked, his fingers continuing their journey through her locks.

"No. At the moment I think that makes me lucky."

"It's debatable which of us is lucky in this moment," he said. His fingers scraped along her scalp, and Alby shivered. Nothing had ever felt so good as Sterling's fingers in her hair. That was her last conscious thought for several hours.

Sometime in the night she woke, startled awake by a chill and the wrongness of her position. The lights were still on. She had fallen asleep sideways on the bed. Similarly, Sterling was asleep beside her, his hand still stretched in her direction. She studied him a moment, smiling fondly. Asleep he looked much more like the boy she had known, all innocence and good cheer. Sterling had been a happy, well-adjusted kid. She debated waking him and sending him to his room but decided against it. It was just Sterling. They'd camped in the same tent before, once when Alby had been inexplicably invited on their senior campout. She stood, retrieved a blanket from the couch, turned off the lights, and lay down again, covering both her and Sterling with the throw. A minute later, she was once again asleep.

CHAPTER 16

When Alby woke the next morning, she was still lying crossways on the bed only now she was plastered to Sterling, her back to his front. Obviously she had wormed her way closer to him in the night like a heat seeking missile. She squeezed her eyes closed, her face flushing with embarrassment. How could she possibly ease away before he woke? There was no way he wouldn't believe she hadn't eased close to him on purpose.

"Hey, you awake?" he whispered.

"Yes," she replied, her tone hesitant.

His hand settled onto her hip, his thumb gliding along her waist. "Don't take this the wrong way." She braced herself, prepared to come up with some excuse as to how they'd wound up in this preposterous position, and then he continued. "But I think that's the best sleep I had in years."

She rolled onto her back. His hand migrated to her stomach, flattening across her belly button. He smiled at her from very nearby. "I should probably warn you I'm kind of a cuddlebug," she whispered.

"In that case I should probably warn you I am, too," he said.

"Are you making fun of me?" she asked.

He rolled onto his back, bringing her with him, tucking her cozily on top of his chest. "How can I prove to you I'm not, Albertine?" His hand smoothed down the length of her back.

"Well, this is a mighty fine start, Sterling," she said. She rested her arms on his chest, surveying his face from very close by. Her finger skimmed along his stubble. "This is something new. Don't believe I've ever seen you anything but clean shaved until lately."

"Here's another secret for you: it took me years to be anything other than a baby face. I used to outright lie about shaving. Truth was, I didn't have to do it until after I graduated college."

"Why would you have to lie about that?"

"It's a guy thing, a matter of pride."

"Well, you have nothing to be ashamed about now," she said, her palm scraping his raspy cheek. He leaned into her touch, smiling.

"You have raccoon eyes," he said, swiping his thumbs beneath her eyes.

"Ugh, don't remind me. I fell asleep before I could wash my makeup off." She started to pull away, to go wash her face and shower, but he held her fast.

"Did I say I didn't like it? You wake up the same as you fall asleep—cute."

"Remind me to thank whoever set your bar so low," she said. He laughed and she smiled. She liked to make Sterling laugh. Previously no one had ever gotten close enough to see her sense of humor before. They thought of her as being sickly sweet, but the truth was that she had a cutting sense of humor. She simply knew better than to let it show most of the time. *Pretty is as pretty does,* had been one of her mother's most loved sayings.

"What's on our agenda today, Miss Mowry?" he asked.

"Golf and a meeting," she said.

"Golf," he groaned. "Not my sport."

"Bet you it is," she said.

"You keep saying that, despite how many times I tell you I'm bad at it."

"Sterling, I spent our entire childhood watching you play sports. Believe me when I tell you there is no way you are as bad at golf as you think you are."

"Are you willing to make a wager on it?" he asked.

"Absolutely. That's how deep my faith in your abilities goes," she said. "What's the wager?"

"Hmm, this is momentous. I'd better take my time and make it worth my while." His thumb smoothed over her lip. "Winner buys the loser dinner and walks him to the door to say goodnight."

"You're really embracing your role as fake boyfriend."

"Sterling Thompson doesn't do anything halfway, which reminds me. Last night I happen to remember telling you there was something we were going to come back to. What was it? Oh, I remember. The fact that you're ticklish."

His hand began to edge toward her neck. Her head snapped to her shoulder, clamping down. "Don't."

"It's a man's prerogative to know exactly how ticklish his woman is, Alby."

"I'm not," she lied. Her chest was doing that panicky thing it did before every time she was tickled, as if opening a floodgate of adrenaline. She kept a wary eye on Sterling's hand, but he went for the sneak attack, leaned up, and bit the exposed part of her neck. Predictably, she screamed and tried to wrench away. Unpredictably, he advanced his attack by rolling her onto her back, pinning her with his weight, and biting her again.

"Don't," she wheezed. "Stop."

"Don't stop? Okay." He dug in, nibbling her relentlessly in the most sensitive spot, the crook of her neck.

"Please," she gasped, desperate for an end to the torture. And then it did end, but not because Sterling stopped touching her. Rather the nature of his touch shifted from relentless biting to gentle nipping and then… "Are…are you kissing my neck?"

He froze. "Yes."

"Why?"

He eased back until they were nose to nose. "It seemed like the thing to do in this situation."

"Oh. So, are we pretending when we're not in front of other people, too?" she whispered.

He grinned. "Absolutely."

"'Kay," she said and tipped her face up, brushing her lips to his. He dipped his head, intending to deepen the kiss, when someone knocked on her door. Hard. They froze.

"What time is it?" she asked.

"Six." He eased away from her and rolled onto his back, freeing her to answer the door. She stood, straightened her rumpled hoodie, reached a hand to her tangled mass of hair, gave up on it, and headed for the door.

"Peter," she exclaimed. Her cousin stood on the other side of the door and, not waiting for an invitation, barreled inside.

"We need to talk."

Alby blinked at him, more than a little startled by his abrupt appearance. "It's six in the morning."

"Yes, well, this is a conversation that needs to happen before the day begins," Peter said.

"Okay," Alby drawled. "Would you care for a cup of coffee?" She moved toward the coffeemaker.

"I'll get it," Sterling offered and Peter jumped.

"Oh, you're here," Peter remarked. Sterling didn't reply as he set about making coffee, but it was obvious that Peter had come to talk about him and had also expected to find Alby alone. "Alby, I'd prefer to have this conversation alone."

"Would you?" Alby replied. She sounded calm, but there was a hint of steel in the words. Sterling thought Peter often forgot Alby was the head of the company, whether this was because she was younger or because she was a woman or because she was naturally kind and laid back he still hadn't determined.

"Yes, it's company business," Peter said, sounding more pompous than important.

"I'll take a shower and leave you to it," Sterling said. He handed Peter his coffee and leaned in to kiss Alby's cheek. They waited to speak until the bathroom door closed with a snap.

"I don't understand what's going on here, Alby," Peter said.

"I don't understand your confusion, Peter," she said.

"You know this merger is important and you show up here with him." He pointed to the bathroom door, as if there were so many men he had to verify the correct one.

"So? You showed up with Gloria," she said.

"She's my *wife*. He's some random employee," Peter said.

"He's not some random employee. I've known him all my life."

"And you decide to debut him here? Do you know how that looks?"

"No, how does it look? Like I'm a normal woman with normal needs and desires? How does this affect you or the company, Peter? I don't understand," Alby said.

"It's not…it's just…it's indecent," Peter finished.

"How?"

"Because you're all over each other like love-starved teenagers," he declared.

"That is completely untrue. You know what I think is going on here?"

"What?"

"I think you had me in some sort of box, one where I was alone, possibly forever. And now that Sterling's in the picture you have to readjust your perception of me."

"My only concern here is for the company," he insisted.

"Then we're on the same page," Alby said, smiling. They stared each other down a few beats.

"Just be careful of this guy. I don't trust him," Peter said at last.

"Funny, that's what he says about you," Alby said. He didn't like that, she could tell. But he'd said his piece and couldn't seem to think of any other reason to stay. With a nod, he finally let himself out. Alby sank to the bed. She felt drained and the day had barely begun.

Sterling opened the door and poked his head out. His dark hair was wet and curly, well-muscled chest and abs exposed. "Is it safe to come out?"

Alby noted the towel tied around his waist. "Safe for who?"

"I forgot to grab clothes from my room." He sat beside her and lightly bumped her shoulder. "Have you been duly warned away from me by your well-meaning cousin who only has your safety at heart?"

"I believe so," she said, resting her head on his shoulder.

"He's probably right, though. I might not be a gold digger, but I'm pretty messed up in all the other ways, Alby."

"We're all a mess, Sterling. Don't be big-headed enough to think your mess is special."

He didn't argue with her further, but it *was* different. Alby was a millionaire; he was poor. Alby was a CEO; he was her employee. Alby was mentally well; he was on medication for depression. "It's like our roles have flipped," he noted. In high school he'd been on top, Alby at the bottom. And now, when it counted most, he was the one looking up. He hated it, and not just because he was the one on the bottom. He hated the disparity between them, hated how much better she was than him now. So far out of his league, though why that should matter when they were merely friends was anybody's guess. He could feel himself sinking, becoming weighted down by obsessive, negative thoughts. *Failure, you are such a failure.*

"Sterling," Alby said, tone soft and serious.

He faced her.

"It's like someone just pulled your plug. What's going on?"

Could he tell Alby the truth? He hadn't dated anyone since his downward spiral began, hadn't had to inform anyone of the broken mess his mind had become. He stared down, rolling the edge of the towel between his fingers. "I, ah, I've been having some trouble with depression."

Her hand rested gently on his shoulder, supportive, encouraging. "Are you doing anything about it?"

He nodded. "I'm taking medication. It helps some. But I still... struggle...now and again. The doctor thinks given my, uh, Dad's situation," he paused and regarded her. She gave him an encouraging nod.

It was a relief, he realized, to be with someone who knew his family's murky history, his dad's struggle with bipolar disorder. "Given the family history, she thinks it might be a chronic condition." He cleared his throat again.

"I'm sorry. That must be very challenging," she said, giving his shoulder a squeeze.

"It felt like…" he broke off, darting a glance at her again. Being with Alby was so easy, so comfortable that it made him say more than he usually might.

"Like what?" she prompted, tone gentle as she rubbed a soothing little circle on his shoulder.

"It felt like I'd been standing on stage my whole life, juggling too many balls. And then I dropped them all. In front of everyone."

"I imagine that's very hard. But guess what?"

"What?" he whispered, body tense and expectant.

She smiled, a kind, reassuring smile. "You're still Sterling Thompson, still as amazing and special and wonderful as always."

She sounded so sincere. No pity, just a normal amount of empathy, tinged with a whole lot of support. "Thanks." His throat felt strangely choked. He cleared it. "So as you can see, I'm not such a good candidate for lifelong love or anything."

"Why on earth not?" she asked, tone vehement.

"What do you mean why not? What woman in her right mind would want to be manacled to a lifetime of mental illness?"

"Well, that's about the dumbest thing I've ever heard, Sterling. It's like saying, 'What woman would want to be manacled to a diabetic' or 'a guy with bad knees' or 'insert any manner of medical scenario.'"

"But it's not the same, not the same at all," Sterling insisted. "I know what it was like to grow up with my dad. It's…it's so hard. I would never want to put a woman through what my mom went through."

"So don't," she said.

"You think I can control it?" he snapped.

"Your depression? No. Not turning into your dad? Yes. I've met your dad a few times, you remember. You're not him," she said.

He blinked, thinking. "That's what my sister says."

She smiled. "How is Birdie? I always liked her."

He smiled, too. "Peas in a pod, the two of you. She's currently working on a cruise ship in the Mediterranean. Guess who she's dating." He elbowed her.

"Erik Estrada."

"What…Alby, my lands, girl. The things that come out of your mouth sometimes. No, she's dating Hayden Paxton."

Alby's mouth puckered into a little O of surprise. "Hayden Paxton. Now there's a name I never thought I'd hear you say without a sneer. I take it you're okay with that?"

"First of all, I had no choice. Second, yeah, I kind of am. He's been really good to her, and good for her. Better than Duncan." He sighed.

She rubbed a little circle on his shoulder once again and, like before, he felt the tension drain out of him.

"Duncan is Duncan," she said.

"Yeah," he agreed, smiling a little. "I love that you know all this and I don't have to explain it or give you the back story." He eased his arms around her and gave her a hug. She slipped her arms around him and hugged him in return, resting her head on his chest.

"Hey, Sterling."

"Yes, Albertine."

"You're pretty naked right now. Not really sure what to do with that," she admitted.

"If we were back in high school, you'd be doing laundry in the locker room right about now," he said. His fingers eased into her hair, sliding along her scalp. She gave a shivery little shudder.

"I'm fresh out of laundry soap at the moment," she whispered. "Hmm, maybe we could…"

Another knock sounded on the door.

"This is getting ridiculous," Sterling said, standing to answer the door. He pulled it open and came face to face with Hart Wentworth who blinked at him in surprise.

"Hi, sorry, I came to see if Alby wanted to grab a cup of coffee before breakfast." His eyes dropped involuntarily to the towel on Sterling's waist before darting away.

Sterling wanted to tell him exactly what he could do with the suggestion. Instead he moved aside, allowing Hart a clear sightline of Alby. "Sweetheart? You in the mood to grab a coffee with Hart here?"

"Gee, that sounds lovely," Alby said in a painfully convincing tone. "But I need to grab a shower right quick. See you at breakfast, maybe?"

"I'll be looking forward to it," Hart said with an unconvincing smile. He nodded at Sterling who returned it and closed the door.

"He's a curious cat," Sterling noted, returning to sit by Alby again.

"How so?"

"There's something almost predatory about him, and yet I don't hate him," Sterling said.

"I think he's merely desperate for the merger to work, being a family company and all."

"Well, I can't fault a man for that. He's me on a grander scale, and we're both at your mercy."

"Sterling, I could just give you the money for your store. Then you could get back to it and you wouldn't have to..." She stopped talking when he pressed his finger to her lips.

"No, baby. It doesn't work like that. I'm not completely a kept man, not yet."

"But I invest in businesses all the time, and I think..."

"Girl, you keep talking, and I'm going to have to think of other ways to shut you up," he warned.

She smiled against his finger. "I think what really needs to happen is that..."

He leaned forward and bit her neck, and she squealed, tossing herself backwards onto the bed to get away from him. He pinned her with one arm and they stared at each other, smiling.

"I don't think I'd be able to do this with anyone else," she noted.

"Staring contest?" he guessed.

"No, this," she brushed a finger over his pec. "Being this close to any other guy with a towel on, and I'd be all flustered and discombobulated, but it's you and I've known you forever and seen you like this lots of times."

"Huh," Sterling said, squinting a little.

"What?"

"Sometimes a guy wants to think he makes a girl discombobulated, Alby."

"Well, I'm sure some girls you do. You're a startlingly handsome man, always have been." She eased her fingers through his hair. "You were always that boy, the one the girls wanted. From middle school on up. And you've gotten better looking with age."

"But you don't think of me that way," he clarified.

"And you don't think of me that way."

"You've got me all sewn up, Albertine." He eased closer and hooked his ankle over her foot, drawing her closer. It was a possessive little action that set her heart out of rhythm a few beats. His hand threaded through hers, palm to palm, and gave it a squeeze.

"How come you call me by my full name now?"

"Cause I like it."

"You cannot like it. It's physically impossible to like the name Albertine."

"But I do. I like it very much." He eased impossibly closer, whispering. "Because..."

The whisper gave her a little chill. It took her a moment to realize he hadn't completed the sentence. "Because why?" He was right there. It was only natural to touch him, and yet her fingers landed on bare skin and hard muscle.

"Nah, forget it. I changed my mind."

"You're teasing me, aren't you?" she asked.

His hand slid to her face, thumb skimming her lip. "Yes."

She rolled toward him, hand gliding over his flat belly. "Well, Sterling, I think you're forgetting something." She tipped forward, lips almost brushing his. He swallowed hard. She smiled.

"What's that?" His voice was a croaky whisper.

"That's my towel." She snapped the knot free, gave a mighty yank

and hopped off the bed, giggling as she locked herself in the bathroom, his towel in hand.

"Albertine," he called, shocked and indignant. "How am I supposed
to walk out of here now?"

"You're a project manager. Manage it." She turned on the shower
and stepped beneath the spray, forcing herself to stop laughing so she
wouldn't drown.

CHAPTER 17

They met up in the hallway some time later.

"I can't hardly believe you," Sterling said, shaking his head at her. "I am shocked, *shocked.*"

"That's what you get for playing with fire. Plus I didn't see anything. Hardly."

"Who's this girl and where's my sweet Alby?" he demanded, leaning forward to give her a peck on the cheek.

She stood on her toes, clutching his shirt to keep her balance. "I don't let her come out when golf is on the table."

"A killer, are you? Too bad you've got me for a partner."

"We'll see. Remember our bet, and no taking a dive on purpose to get out of it," she said.

"Baby, I don't know the meaning of the words. One of us actually does have a killer instinct, and I'm fairly certain it's me. But I'm also telling you I've golfed before. Don't expect good things."

"I always expect good things from you, Sterling, and you always deliver."

"Alby, Alby, Alby. What am I going to do with you?" He snagged an arm around her waist and led her toward the elevator. His phone buzzed and he pulled it out. "It's Bess. She wants to know how we're doing. Lean in here, we'll send her a selfie." They put their heads together. He snapped the picture and sent it to Bess. She replied a minute later.

*H*MM. *Looks like a match.*

S*TERLING REPLIED*. *Nah, she's way out of my league.*

*I'*M BEGINNING *to believe it. Then again, who would be good enough? Better you than someone unknown who might not keep her safe. Something to ponder.*

"W*HAT*?" Alby asked, watching him stare thoughtfully at his phone.

He shoved it in his pocket. "I want things to work for Bess and Hogue. She needs her happy ending and, never thought I'd say it, but I think Hogue might be it."

"What do you think would help them?" she asked.

"Being marooned on a desert island with ample time to talk and work through their problems."

"Is that all? Leave it to me," she said, smiling a little secret smile.

"I like it when you're ornery, Miss Mowry," he said, tipping her face and brushing a kiss on her nose as the doors opened, spilling them into the middle of the dining room. Everyone was already there, Hart, Whitney, Peter, Gloria, and all her employees. Alby blushed and straightened, but Sterling didn't react. They hadn't done anything wrong. More importantly, Alby was the head of the company. If she wanted to fling him onto a table and kiss him senseless, she could. In fact, he was beginning to wish she would.

"Why you smiling like that?" she whispered.

"You really don't want to know," he said, tossing her a wink.

"Oh, boy," she muttered, cheeks flushing.

He reached around her for a fork, pausing to whisper. "Why, Albertine, are you feeling a bit discombobulated?"

She tipped her face toward him. "I don't know, Sterling. Are you?"

His lashes fluttered. "I think maybe I am."

She laughed as if he'd said something funny, when really he'd never been more earnest. Alby was taking him by surprise in all the ways lately. They retrieved their breakfast and sat at a table with Hart and Whitney. Their easy camaraderie made Sterling yearn for Birdie. He needed to have a chat with her soon. Would he tell her about the new developments with Alby? Perhaps not yet. Everything felt a bit too new and vulnerable for that. Then again, what didn't feel vulnerable lately? Sterling's entire life felt like an exercise in peeling back layers.

"Good morning," Whitney said cheerfully. "It's nice to see you, though according to Hart I already missed the show." She shot Sterling a cheeky little grin.

"I hope it was a good one," Sterling said easily. Of all the things he had to be insecure about, his body wasn't one.

"I'm sure it was, but I guess Alby's the final authority," Whitney said, and now all attention swung to Alby, awaiting her verdict.

"Well, Sterling has always known what looks best on him," she said, giving his leg a pat.

"Ah, sounds like we both like our men brawny and submissive," Whitney said, shooting her a conspiratorial smile.

"I'm not certain anyone would ever classify Sterling Thompson as submissive, but the brawn part stands," Alby said loyally. Under the table, Sterling gave her leg a squeeze. Alby would never be one to take potshots at another person for her own amusement or adulation. It was yet one more thing to appreciate about her on an ever-growing list.

"Aren't you two just the cutest?" Whitney said, venom in the deepest depths of her tone.

"We're definitely in the running, but I think you need to wear matching outfits or costumes to win," Sterling said. "I'm game, but Alby's strangely hesitant."

"I just don't think matching kilts are the way to go," Alby returned and Sterling sputtered a laugh, taking a gulp of coffee to avoid choking.

"Hmm." Whitney's eyes darted between them. "I was talking to Peter this morning, and he had no idea you two were together until last night."

"That is strange," Sterling agreed. "Usually I keep my distant cousin apprised of all my romantic goings on. Can't imagine why Alby didn't." He tossed her a look and an exaggerated shrug. She smiled placidly in return and buttered her toast.

"You'll have to forgive my sister," Hart inserted, giving Whitney's shoulder a warning squeeze. "She's recently out of a relationship and feeling a bit bitter about love."

"Oh, I'm so sorry," Alby said sincerely.

"If it's any consolation, I was coming out of a pretty bitter breakup when Alby and I got together, proving you never know where and when love can strike."

"How charming," Hart said with zero sincerity. He leaned forward and addressed Alby. "I hear you're a pretty avid golfer, Miss Mowry."

Alby tipped her head to him with a coy smile, refusing to brag or incriminate herself if she was awful. "Is she?" Whitney demanded of Sterling.

"I have no idea. We've never golfed together," Sterling said.

"Sterling's good," Alby declared.

"Girl, I am not," he argued. She nodded. He shook his head. She poked him.

"Would you care to make a little wager on the day?" Hart inserted.

"What'd you have in mind?" Alby asked, swiveling her attention to him.

"If you win, I will donate ten thousand dollars of my personal money to the charity of your choice," he said.

"And if you win?" she asked.

"You'll buy my company outright, no more pussyfootin' or negotiations."

She regarded him, stirring her coffee idly. Sterling shifted, holding his breath. "That's quite a disparity, ten thousand dollars versus twenty five million."

Sterling almost swallowed his tongue. Twenty five million? He knew Alby had money, that her company was doing well, but he had no idea she had twenty five million in capital at her disposal.

"I'd say it's pretty consistent with where we are in the world, in terms of net worth. And my money would be going to some charity that's meaningless to me. Yours would net a profit over time," Hart reasoned.

Alby stirred a few more times, staring at him, then extended her hand over the table to shake. "Deal."

"Aren't you going to check with your boyfriend here?" Whitney asked and Hart shot her a look that made her press her lips together. Sterling could practically read his mind. *We have her where we want her, dummy. Don't ruin it.*

"I can't imagine a scenario where Alby would have to check with me about business decisions. As I stated before, it's her company to do with what she will."

"I've found that men generally can't help themselves from expressing an opinion on financial matters."

"Maybe so, if they have a valid opinion. But I am, by every single definition, a business failure. And Alby is clearly very much not. I would defer to her every time and twice on Sundays." Sterling picked up his coffee and tipped it toward Alby in a silent toast. He wasn't being hyperbolic, and they both knew it. She was a CEO and seasoned businesswoman. He was the owner of a failed bookstore and temporary project manager. Why anyone thought he would offer her unsolicited advice was a mystery.

"You two are all kinds of fascinating to me," Whitney said, the first truly sincere statement she'd made since they met her, Sterling thought.

"Why? Because she's worth a thousand of me in every possible way?" Sterling asked.

"Sterling," Alby said, annoyed now.

"So many reasons," Whitney said. "For one thing the fact that y'all went to school together and only now started dating."

"I had a lot of growing up to do," Sterling said sincerely. "I still do. Haven't you ever looked at someone and seen them differently, all of a sudden?" Again, he was telling the honest truth. Previously he had been too young and stupid to understand what a treasure Alby was, how necessary her brand of loyalty and kindness were in the world. She was like the first snowfall, covering everything in a layer of pureness and white. He reached out and gave her neck a little a squeeze, smiling. She looked adorable in her little golf outfit, hair up in a perky ponytail.

"Look at you, lookin' at her," Whitney interjected. "Somebody oughta snap a picture."

"We should probably get started," Hart said, pointedly ignoring his sister. Yesterday they had seemingly been on the same page, but today things were different. Sterling wondered why. What had skewed Whitney another direction? Suddenly he wished for Duncan, the first time he'd done so in weeks, since learning of his betrayal. But Duncan was a good wingman and good at handling crazy women, women like Whitney. Probably because he never let his heart get involved, kept himself aloof. Women like Whitney, pretty, rich women who were used to being adored, could never resist the challenge of trying to be the one who landed him. Little did they know his heart already belonged to one Birdie Thompson, currently a world away in Italy.

Sterling, on the other hand, did not do well with women like Whitney. He liked women in need of a savior. Somehow he ended up being the hero of every relationship. He tossed a glance toward Alby, after an uncomfortable realization. He had preemptively made himself her savior by staging the fake relationship. Whether it was a necessity or not, he would now never know. He snagged her around the neck and leaned in to whisper.

"Remind me I owe you an apology later."

She blinked up at him, puzzled. "For what?"

"Probably a few things, starting with the twenty five million you're about to lose. Alby, I am not good at golf."

She eased her arm around his waist. "Sterling, you're good at everything."

He felt a familiar panicky sensation in his chest. *Not now, go away,* he pled. Now was so not the time for an anxiety attack. His meds kept him pretty even keel, until they didn't. And then an episode could be epic. *I am not responsible for Alby's business dealings,* he reminded himself. *She made the deal on her own, not based on my ability to win at golf. All I can do is my best.*

Alby squeezed his waist and whispered. "Hey, it's just for fun. Win or lose, I don't care."

"Honestly?" he said.

"I promise," she said, rubbing a soothing little circle on his shoulder. Somehow that magic little touch released the pressure on his anxiety valve and he felt himself relax.

"But it's twenty five million dollars," he whispered.

"Believe it or not, that's a bargain price. Although if I do decide to buy, I'd like to get him down to eighteen."

"Who are you, Albertine?" he whispered.

"I'm the same girl I've always been," she replied.

"What took me so long to see you?" he mused, more to himself than her.

They picked up their caddies and golf cart. Sterling was the only one who had to rent clubs. He supposed he should feel embarrassed by that, but this was only his third time golfing. The rarity of the act made dropping a small fortune on a nice set seem ridiculous. Especially when he had so many other pressing financial needs in his life.

Hart and Whitney shared a look when he received his bag of rented clubs. In their world it was unheard of to rent. Everyone probably had their own horse and European sports car, too. In Sterling's world people were lucky to own their own small home, to be able to place food on the table each night and buy Christmas presents for their kids. He comforted himself that Alby was far more comfortable and familiar with his world than she was with theirs. She might be a millionaire, but she had never lived like one. She'd been raised in their small, poverty-stricken town, not among the social elite of Atlanta. He wondered if she felt as out of place as he did and clasped her hand, giving it an encouraging squeeze. She smiled up at him. Her eyes were the most interesting shade of amber, perfectly set against her auburn hair. He lifted her hand and brushed a kiss on her knuckles.

"For luck," he explained.

"You ooze charm," she accused.

"Sorry, I've been meaning to have that looked at," he returned. She laughed, he smiled, and they both realized Whitney and Hart were waiting on them.

"Ladies first," Hart said, standing graciously aside so Alby could move forward.

Her caddie handed her a ball and club. She took a stance and swung, slicing a clean shot that, to Sterling's amateurish eyes, looked like a good one. Hart whistled appreciatively, confirming his opinion.

"That's a killer," Hart said. "Let's hope Whit has one like that in her."

Whitney had the toned body of an athlete and seemed comfortable on the course. She took her shot and they all squinted to see where it might land.

"Well, the ladies are setting us up for a good day. Sterling, go right ahead," Hart said, motioning for Sterling to move forward. His caddie handed him a ball and club and he tried not to be nervous while he got himself arranged. He had only ever golfed with Duncan, for fun. Now he wished he had tried harder or paid more attention as he played with three people who had been doing it all their lives and likely had lessons. Duncan had taken a few lessons when he was a kid, which was where all of Sterling's knowledge came from. He tried to channel it and remember now as he took a breath and swung.

"Not half bad," Hart said cheerfully, which Sterling took to mean wasn't half good, either. While Hart set up his shot, Sterling took out his phone and surreptitiously texted Duncan.

· · ·

NEED all your best golf knowledge ASAP.

DON'T mix plaids with stripes, Duncan returned.

SERIOUS STUFF. A big bet on the line. Help, Sterling sent.

The good thing about having the same best friend all his life was that they'd developed a pretty good shorthand. Duncan understood his advice was critical and boiled down everything he knew, texting it in snippets so that by the time it was Sterling's turn to hit again, he had a better memory of what do to.

"Hmm," Hart noted after Sterling's second stroke landed on the green. His dismal tone told Sterling it had been a good shot, a notion confirmed when he came in one under par on the hole.

Alby sidled up to him and sniffed. "Is that victory I smell?"

"If the penalty is dinner with you, it's a victory either way, Alby," Sterling replied. Maybe it was because he was euphoric over doing better than he thought he might at golf. Whatever the reason, he was overcome with the mad desire to tug her close and kiss her like he meant it. Of course he couldn't, though. It wasn't the sort of thing people did in the middle of golf, and especially not at a four star resort. But the inability to complete the thought rumbled through him, giving him a burst of much needed adrenaline. His dormant competitive streak awoke, jolting through him like the warm up before every football game. *We're going to win this,* he thought. *We're going to win this for Alby and all the times she hasn't won before.* For once Albertine Mowry would know how it felt to be on the winning team, not on the sidelines handing out water bottles, not in the locker room washing towels. A winner.

What? she mouthed, sensing the shift in him.

He wagged his brows at her. Her smile widened, showing the hint of a dimple he'd never noticed before. His eyes remained on her a few beats too long. *I'm mooning. Over Alby. And I like it.*

The remainder of the morning shifted from lighthearted to cutthroat and for the first time Sterling was glad he'd inserted himself into Alby's scenario. She and Whitney were evenly matched as far as golf went. But Whitney was bitingly sarcastic and vindictively cruel when she thought she could get away with it. With Sterling there, she couldn't get away with it. Alby might be content to let the cattiness slide, to either pretend not to hear it or greet it with a bland smile. But Sterling called her on it every time. Pausing to stare at her unblinking, calling her out without using words, making her squirm with guilt and shame. Eventually the remarks tapered off until they stopped altogether.

But while Whitney began behaving like a proper human being, her brother devolved into a competitive caveman. His ire was only directed at Sterling and therefore manageable and amusing. First he stopped being magnanimous. "I believe it's your turn, Sterling, old man," turned into, "You going to go or what?" Until at last he stopped speaking all together, squinting in concentration.

In the end, Sterling golfed the best game of his life. Whitney beat Alby by one stroke, but Alby and Sterling won by five strokes. Hart picked up one of his very expensive golf clubs, intending to hurl it like a javelin, when Alby put a hand on his bicep.

"The weekend's not over, Mr. Wentworth. Only the game of golf. We still have a lot to discuss, I think."

Hart studied her, hand gripping the iron like a claw, until eventually he took a deep breath and forced a smile. "You're right of course, Alby. Please forgive me. I get a mite competitive."

"It's all right, I know how that goes," Alby said, linking her arm with Sterling and tossing him a smile. Sterling wondered if she was remembering the time he and Hayden Paxton got into a brawl in the locker room after a particularly nasty playoff loss.

"Why don't you all take the cart? Alby and I are going to take a slight detour," Sterling said.

"Sounds fair. We'll drop these rental clubs off for you," Hart offered.

"I'd appreciate that," Sterling said, deciding not to read anything offensive in the subtext of his tone. They waved them away and he turned Alby toward the resort's lush garden.

"What are we doing?" Alby asked, double stepping to keep up with his long strides.

He reached for her hand, anchoring her beside him. "We're looking for something."

"What?" she asked.

"This." He led her behind a massive royal oak, its sprays of Spanish moss obscuring them from view.

"Why?"

"So we can do this victory dance." He tossed her over his shoulder and spun in a circle while she laughed. He set her down and pressed her against the tree, being careful to avoid the chigger-ridden moss. "Thank you for a fun morning."

"Thank you for winning at golf."

"Thank you for believing I could," he returned.

"You're good at all the things," she said, resting her hands on his belt and giving it a little tug.

"It's nice you think so. How are you feeling about your upcoming meeting this afternoon? Ready for them to woo you?"

"I think so. I have all the stats. Peter and our accounting department have raked their records over the coals. All that's left is to hear Hart's personal plea."

"He wants it so bad he can taste it," Sterling said.

"I reckon so," she agreed.

"If you buy him out, are you prepared to handle him? Because he's not going to go away. He's going to dog your steps, wanting to have final say and approval on everything."

"I don't know. I have considered that, of course. The truth is I'm not certain I can handle him on any sort of sustained basis. His company is solid, but he's my drawback. I don't want to spend the rest of my life fighting him over every decision."

"On the other hand, I think he's taken an actual shine to you, more than trying to suck up and impress you. The way you handled him this morning was about more than the company. You got to him."

"I know a thing or two about overly competitive athletes," she said.

"You're pretty good at handling me, too. You take me outside of myself, get me out of my head. It's, well, it's a huge relief the way you're able to do that. Sort of short-circuit my brain's faulty wiring. Birdie's the same way."

Her smile dimmed slightly and he wondered why. Because she wasn't the only woman with the ability to soothe him or because he'd compared her to his sister?

"I should get back. I need to freshen up before my meeting."

"Me, too," he agreed. While she met with the bigwigs, he would meet with the other project managers.

They faced the resort and started to walk. Sterling took her hand, giving it a squeeze. "It's pretty here. Soothing. It's been nice to get away and have a change of scenery. Thank you."

She smiled, cheeks flushing. "You're welcome. You're the only one who has thanked me. I think the others might see it as a drudge."

"They don't, not at all. I've heard several of them comment how great it is to be here, to get away and be able to work in this sort of environment. But that's how it is with bosses. There has to be a line between or else it gets weird."

"This is some line," she said, holding their linked hands aloft between them.

"I'm not a real employee. I'm a glorified temp. My interest in you is purely personal." He brought her hand to his lips and kissed it. They reached the resort and stepped into the elevator. He deposited her in front of her door. "Good luck in your meeting."

"Thanks. I think I'm going to need it."

He drew her into a crushing hug. "No, you won't because you're crazy smart and capable and wise and the best person I've ever known. You're going to make the right decision because you always do, and it's going to be great." He felt a little bit of the tension drain out of her at his words. He rubbed a soothing little circle on her back and she melted, pressing into him.

"That's so nice."

"The words or the backrub?" he asked.

"All of it."

He kissed her forehead. "I should let you go." But he didn't. They remained canoodled in the hallway until they finally had to dash inside and sprint around getting ready for their respective meetings.

CHAPTER 18

"Everybody shh, Dad's here."

The whispered aside was said loudly enough for Sterling to hear, on purpose he was certain. He smiled. "That's right, everybody get it out of your systems."

"You could have told us from the beginning you were a ringer," Sheila said.

"I'm not. Alby and I weren't together when I got hired."

"So you started dating after she became your boss? Nice," Al said, holding his hand up for a high five no one returned.

"Alby and I have known each other our whole lives," Sterling said. "I have the pictures to prove it. I spent half my teenage years at her house, every Friday night football game she was there. Every party after the game was at her house. Every social outing, Alby was involved." When he thought about it, Alby was on the fringe of every school memory he had.

"So this has been building for a long time, is what you're saying. Like you always had a secret crush? On *Alby*?" Al asked.

Sterling shrugged. He didn't owe these people anything and neither did Alby. Especially not her, since she was the one paying their salaries. "The point is my relationship with Alby has nothing to do with my job. She's still my boss, and yours too, I might point out."

"Narc," Al coughed.

Now Sterling was getting annoyed because the mood bordered on disrespect to Alby. "That's right, I am. My first and only loyalty will always be to Alby. So I guess if you don't want me telling tales to your boss, maybe we should get to work." It was his deadly tone more than his words that convinced them. Their conspiratorial wink, wink, nudge, nudge smiles disappeared as they turned their focus to work.

In the conference room next door, Alby wasn't faring as well. Hart gave his pitch, an earnest assessment of why she should buy his company, starting with its founding three generations ago and detailing all the families they'd supported over the years, including his own. It was clear he thought she would be swayed by the emotion of it all, and she was. She loved that it was a family company, like hers. But, as Sterling had pointed out, theirs wouldn't be a merger of numbers. It would be a marriage of two family companies. How would that work? Would he fight her on everything for the remainder of their merger? Or would it be more insidious? She could see Peter hanging on Hart's every word, eager to approve the sale. Suddenly she wondered why. Did Peter think if Hart joined on, they could make it a boys' club and override her? And then there was Whitney to consider, openly hostile and vaguely threatening for reasons Alby didn't understand. Did she sense some weakness in Alby that made her want to dominate?

Alby's phone was set to vibrate during the meeting. She received a text and glanced at it absently. Bess had sent a note, as if in answer to a prayer.

STERLING TOLD me about that Whitney girl. Want me to come there and kick her around for you?

. . .

ALBY PICKED up her phone and sent a quick text while Hart's back was turned. *I'd rather understand her motivation. Why does she seem to hate me, even though she doesn't know me?*

BECAUSE YOU'RE HAPPY. And it pokes at all the parts of her that aren't happy. You're CEO, with Sterling, respected, and content. Best advice? Ignore her. It'll drive her crazy and eventually she'll give up and go away. Hart's the real danger there.

ALBY SET her phone aside and studied the back of Hart Wentworth. He was a devastatingly handsome man. The raw material wasn't as attractive as Sterling, but he was more put together, as someone who'd been raised with a silver spoon in his mouth tends to be. It was likely his haircuts cost as much as Sterling's car payments and he probably received facials and manicures, too. But peel away all those layers, and he and Sterling were the same—two men who were trying hard to save their businesses. Sterling took on a job he didn't actually want in order to keep his small business afloat. Hart was attempting to prostrate himself and beg for Alby's help. How would Sterling feel if he had to do that? *He would hate it. It would bring him low, lower than he'd ever been.*

And suddenly she knew what to do. If Whitney was Bess in their world and Hart was Sterling, she was still Alby, would always be Alby, and that was perfectly okay.

"I'd like to speak with Hart a moment alone, please," she said quietly when his spiel was finished. He looked drained, exhausted, defeated, and she kind of hated it. Now that she'd made the comparison between him and Sterling, she couldn't stop overlaying them in her mind.

"I really don't think that's a good idea," Peter interjected.

"I really didn't ask your opinion," Alby returned, startling him so he blinked at her, affronted. Whitney snickered. Like Bess, she seemingly enjoyed it when Alby showed a bit of spirit. They were odd, contradictory women, completely unlike Alby in every possible way. She waited to speak until everyone was out of the room, then patted the seat beside her. Hart sank into it reluctantly, uncertain what to expect.

"Thank you for your presentation," she began. "I can imagine it was an immense amount of work to put together, along with this weekend for my staff. Thank you for hosting and showing us a good time."

"You're welcome, but why does this feel like a rejection?" he asked. He aimed for a lighthearted tone and failed mightily.

"It's not, it's a reciprocation. You laid everything on the line for me, so I'm laying it on the line for you. I like your company, both the numbers you put out and the people you represent. But I have no desire to spend the remainder of my days locked in some kind of *Game of Thrones* duel for supremacy."

"I'm not certain I follow," Hart said slowly. "Is this about Whit? Because I can keep a better leash on her."

"Can you?" Alby smiled. "Somehow I doubt it. But it's not about Whitney. It's about you and me. If I buy your company, I need you to understand that you would be ceding control. It would no longer be your company alone to do with as you please. My massive influx of cash comes with me at the helm. I may seem soft and gentle, and for the most part I am. But push me into a corner, and I'll bite and bite hard. If you start to fight me on things and it becomes a battle, you will be out, just like that. I won't take sentimentality or your family's history with the company into consideration. So if we do this, you need to understand how it's going to be."

He squirmed, annoyed. "What? You want me to roll over and play dead so you can pat my tummy? Feed your ego by deferring to you, even when I disagree?"

"Of course not. But you can't disagree for the sake of disagreement, to maintain power. As of this moment, you have none. I will value your input as someone who understands your company. I will listen to you with due regard. But I will not enter into a power struggle or battle of wills. Part of what makes me a successful businesswoman is that I don't put up with any of that nonsense. This is my one and only warning to you. You're an alpha male, used to being in charge and getting your way. But I also think you genuinely care about your company and your employees. If you want them to succeed, you're going to have to set aside your ego and realize you will work for me from now on, and not the other way around. So I guess what I'm asking, Hart, is if you're man enough to have a female boss and be okay with it?"

If he'd answered right away, she would have been suspicious. But he didn't. He sat staring at his hands a minute, mind working through all the possibilities and ramifications until at last he spoke slowly. "I can't promise I'll get it perfect, but I can promise to try. I like you, Alby, I do. It would be impossible not to. And what's more, I respect you. Everything I've ever heard about you confirms that you are a good, solid, upstanding person and an even better boss. I've been in charge for a lot of years, same as you. My dad brought me up at his knee, preparing me to take the helm. It pains me that I haven't been able to sustain it."

"I haven't been able to find any recklessness or fault on your part, Hart. There's a bit of luck involved in these things. We've had luck on our side. We might not always. Someday it might be me with my hat in hand, asking a bigger company for a bailout. There's no shame in it."

He gave her a sad little smile. "You're kind."

"I can be. But I can also be ruthless."

"Me too, when called for. But I can also be a team player and, I think most of my employees would tell you, humble when called for. If I wasn't willing to swallow a bit of pride, I wouldn't have come calling on you for help. I realized when I reached out I likely wouldn't get to stay at the helm. It's more important to me that the company stays solvent than I'm the one calling the shots."

"Then let's do this," she said. He beamed at her. They shook hands and called everyone back in to go over the particulars.

A long, long time later, Alby let herself into her room. They'd worked through supper, setting up the restructuring and signing over all the many legalities. She wondered what Sterling did for food and where he was now and, with a jolt, realized she missed him. Kind of a lot.

When she flicked on the light, she saw him stretched out on her bed, smiling up at her. "Hey, how'd it go?" He was the handsomest man she'd ever seen in real life. Most girls at school had thought Duncan edged him out in looks, but Duncan had been cold and aloof, far too conceited to ever take seriously. Sterling had always been easier to talk to, his face usually lit by a smile.

She jumped onto the bed, landing beside him with a little plop. "Good."

He wrapped his arms around her and rolled onto his back, taking her with him. "Did you eat?"

"Yes."

"Are you tired?"

"Exhausted. How about you?"

"I ate, but I napped while I waited for you. Objectively I know our mattresses are the same, but I think your bed is more comfy." His hand smoothed over her head and Alby closed her eyes, leaning into his touch, her head resting on his chest. Her family had been touchy-feely, her parents highly affectionate and loving. They'd hugged every day of her life, and then suddenly they were gone. She was left alone and hugless. Touching Sterling, and being touched in return, felt like sensory overload and she loved it. "I missed you."

Her eyes popped open. "Did you really?"

"Why do you say it like that? Like I might be trying to put one over on you. Of course really. We've been inseparable lately. Turns out I like it."

She rested her head on his chest again, hugging him. Lately everything he said left her feeling vaguely and slightly disappointed and she had no idea why. What did she expect him to say? That he'd missed her because she was the love of his life? She thought of all the women he'd dated, the beauties like Bess who knew exactly how to bring men to their knees. Next to them she was the same mouse she'd always been. He rubbed a soothing little circle on her back. "Want me to go?" he whispered.

She sat up. "No. Unless you want to."

He shook his head. "You're keeping me on the ropes here. Did you buy them out or tell them no? Or, third option, you're still thinking about it."

"Guess."

"Hmm." He studied her face, tipping his head. "I honestly don't know. You have a good poker face, Albertine." His fingers trailed through her hair and she rested her head on his chest again, too relaxed to hold it up this time.

"That feels so nice. I love it when you do that."

"I love to do it," he said and gave her a little nudge. "The company."

She smiled against his chest. "I bought it."

"I bet you got him down to eighteen, huh?"

"Eighteen and a half. I had to give him something for his ego after we creamed him at golf."

"A half million ought to do it," he said, his hand once again rubbing her back. Alby squirmed, struggling to get impossibly closer. One of his legs hooked over hers, and her heart started to thump. *It's only pretend,* she reminded herself. *Sterling is playing a part.* They were friends, first, foremost, and forevermore. She had never let herself have feelings for Sterling because he'd always inhabited a different realm. Why lately did it feel like those realms were beginning to inter-sect? "Alby."

"Hmm."

"You seem so tense. What's wrong?"

She eased her head up and rested her elbows on his impressive chest. His brow was furrowed with concern. Why was it so easy to say the things she wanted to say to Hart and so hard with Sterling? "You know what it is, Sterling?"

He shook his head. His face was still puckered in worry, but it did nothing to dim his ridiculous good looks. Between him and Duncan it was as if they'd siphoned all the attractive male DNA in the county, and yet only Duncan had seemed cognizant of the effect they'd had on girls. He'd had a love 'em and leave 'em attitude, flying through a stream of girls at a steady rate. Sterling had always been boyfriend material, Mr. Commitment. Tender, attentive, sensitive, affectionate. He was that guy who could make girls trample each other trying to catch a bouquet at a wedding, if only he could be the guaranteed groom. And now he held Alby tight in his grasp, all his tender attention focused on her.

"It's just…it's that…I…" She was out of words, mostly because she didn't know what they should be. This was Sterling Thompson. She was Albertine Mowry. The gulf between them felt immense, and yet she had never been physically closer to a person than she was at this moment. Even Hogue, when they'd shared their pubescent makeout sessions, hadn't held her this way.

"Hey, Alby," Sterling whispered. His hand caressed her face, thumb tracing the outline of her lips. He swallowed hard, and it was that swallow that convinced her he was as befuddled as she was. His phone rang, an incessant trill. He flinched.

"Do you need to get that?" she whispered.

"It's my ex-girlfriend, Chelsea."

"Is she the one who cheated with Duncan?"

He nodded.

"Did you love her?"

He shook his head. "She calls occasionally to say sorry, to check in, to say she wants to get back together."

"Do you want to get back together?"

He shook his head again, his hands sifting the ends of her hair.

"You look very sad right now," she noted, hands cupping his face.

"Sad was the farthest thing from my mind a moment ago," he said. "But it's not Chelsea."

"Duncan?" she guessed. He nodded. "You two were always a pair, hard to imagine one without the other. It must have been very painful for you when you found out what he did."

"Like a death. I've tried to let it go and move on, but nothing is the same. There's this space between us where there's never been a space before."

"Maybe the trick is for time to work its magic and things will be okay eventually."

"That's the thing, I'm not certain I want them to. Duncan is so… he's…well, you know exactly how Duncan is."

"Yes, I do. He's spoiled and entitled and self-involved."

"To begin with," Sterling agreed, tone bitter.

"But I have a secret about Duncan."

"Please don't tell me you made out with him, too," he said, grimacing.

"Ha, I wish," she said and laughed when his jaw clenched. "I'm joking. I have never been attracted to Duncan, pretty as he is."

She yelped when he flipped her, pinning her beneath him and twining their fingers together. "What's your secret, Albertine? Tell me quick before I decide to tickle you."

"When my parents died, Duncan showed up at my house."

"He did?" Sterling asked, shocked. For years he and Duncan seemingly did nothing without the other, had hardly existed outside the realm of their tight friendship. And he had said nothing about visiting Alby; Sterling would have remembered.

"Yes, he did. He said with most people he would bring a bottle of wine and get drunk, but he knew I didn't drink. So you know what he brought me?"

"No idea," Sterling said, intrigued.

"Hot cocoa. It was the sweetest thing. And he insisted on making it. We sat at my kitchen table and drank cocoa while I talked about my parents. And then when the cocoa was finished, he hugged me hard and let me cry for a while. And then he went home. It was, hands down, one of the nicest things anyone has ever done for me."

Sterling was speechless. He had no idea Duncan had ever done anything so thoughtful and heartfelt for another person. On the one hand it was heartening and he was glad his friend had been there for Alby in her time of need. On the other hand it was maddening. Why had he never shown Sterling that same sort of sensitivity? Why did it seem like Sterling only saw his worst traits lately? He didn't realize he said it out loud until Alby answered.

"Maybe it's the same reason kids misbehave the worst for their parents, because they know they can. You're his person. You've always been his person. I'm not saying he doesn't need to shape up and fix some things, I'm merely offering a reason why he might have behaved the way he has lately. You're his comfort, you and Birdie. You know he told me about her, that night."

"Four years ago?" Sterling exclaimed. He thought Duncan's feelings for Birdie were something new.

She caressed his face, soothing him. "I take it you didn't know."

"Only recently. Why did he keep it hidden for so long? Back then we might have had a chance to make it work. Hayden Paxton would have been a footnote if Duncan and Birdie were already together. He and Chelsea never would have happened."

"Maybe Duncan and Birdie were never meant to be. Maybe Hayden and Birdie were. Who knows how these things happen? I don't, but I'd like to believe we end up with who we're supposed to, when we're supposed to."

Sterling studied her, a slow smile spreading. "Maybe so, Albertine."

Alby might have gulped. The way he was looking at her, what did it mean? One thing was certain, no one had ever looked at her that way before. He rolled to the side, still keeping their joined hands between them. Alby rolled onto her side, facing him. With his free hand, he reached out and brushed the hairs off her face.

"Hey, Alby."

"Yes, Sterling." Her heart thumped hard.

"I think you're pretty great."

Oh. Certain brands of dishwashers were pretty great. "Thank you."

"And also kind of shockingly hot for someone so sweet," he added, nudging closer.

"Yes?" she said, voice going to a faint squeak. She was absolutely certain no one had ever called her hot before.

"Uh, yeah. When I showed up at the welcome ball and saw you, I thought…"

"You thought…" she prompted when he stopped talking.

His eyes skimmed over her face, followed by his finger. "I thought who is that amazing body with that incredible auburn hair? Then I realized it was you and I…"

"And you," she prompted again, a whisper this time.

"And I thought 'Of course it's Alby. She's the total package.' And I'm sorry I inserted myself into your weekend by pretending to be your boyfriend."

"You are?"

He nodded. "You didn't need me. You had this weekend all sewn up on your own. You're capable and strong and put together, able to handle all the things."

"Maybe," Alby began, twisting his shirt in her hand as she edged closer. "But maybe I wanted you to insert yourself." He smiled. Have mercy, he had the best smile she had ever seen. It was a ridiculous combination of masculine angles, beard stubble, and a dimple. Alby had always loved his smile, always thought it was the sweetest thing. But it had never been directed at her before. It was like standing in the path of an F5 tornado. She was toast.

"What would you think if I kissed you?" he whispered.

"I probably wouldn't because then I would be tempted to over-think. I'd probably just go with it and kiss you back," she said. "Or I could kiss you first, save us both the trouble of thinking." She edged forward and brushed her lips to his. He gripped her waist and dragged her closer and Alby realized she was prophetic because from the moment their lips touched, the time for thinking was over.

CHAPTER 19

Sterling's phone trilled, the shrill sound making them jump.

"Is that Chelsea again?" she asked, lips moving against his.

"No. Also, if you could not mention my ex-girlfriend's name while we're making out, that would be great." She laughed and he smiled, all without breaking stride. Their teeth clicked together, which should have been gross but somehow only worked to increase their fervor. The phone stopped ringing, only to immediately start again.

"What if it's your mom?" Alby whispered, cupping his face in her hands, drawing him impossibly closer.

"My mom is also on the list of people not to mention when I'm doing my best to kiss you senseless," he said. His lips migrated to her neck. The phone stopped and started again.

"Sterling," she said, tapping his shoulder. He paused and sagged.

"It's Duncan," he said, easing away to see her face.

"Does he usually call?" she asked.

"No, he always texts."

"That means it's important," she said. She lunged for his phone, mashing him into the bed. His hands were not idle in the interim. She pushed them away and shoved his phone into them instead. "Call your boy. He needs you for something."

"It had better be important," he said, then repeated it again when Duncan picked up. He listened for a minute, spoke a few words, and set the phone aside. "Where were we?"

"You were about to tell me what's up with Duncan," she prodded, poking his shoulder.

He captured her finger. "Apparently Chelsea's in labor."

She shot upward. "What? That's a big deal. What else did he say?"

"How do you know these things?" he said.

"Maybe because I've known you since we were five or maybe because you look all squirmy, like you're trying to hide something from me."

"Your magic is powerful. Duncan is heading to the hospital to be there for the birth and he's freaking out. He wants me to come."

She rolled off the bed. "I'll help you pack."

"Alby, I can't go," he stared at her aghast.

"Sterling, you can't not go," she returned, hands on hips.

He sat up. "They cheated on me. What kind of guy shows up for the birth of his ex-girlfriend's baby with another guy, his best friend?"

"The really good kind who is there for his lifelong friend, even when he's been a complete..." she broke off, searching for the best descriptor.

Sterling grinned, waiting her out. He had never heard Alby say anything bad about anyone before. He was preemptively amused by whatever she might come up with.

"Toad," she finished with a satisfied nod.

"Toad? That's it? That's all you've got?" he asked.

"I like Duncan. He didn't cheat on *me*," she said. She went back to the bed and pulled him into a hug, cradling his face against her stomach. "And while I am very sorry he cheated on you, I also know you. Someday you're going to regret it if you're not there for this."

He hugged her hard and pressed his ear to her belly button, oddly soothed by the soft murmur of her heart. "Could you come with me?"

"If you want," she said, smoothing her hand over his head.

"I want, I very much want," he said, then felt immediate guilt. She wasn't like other women, wasn't free to drop everything to attend to his whims. "But I know how important this weekend is to you. Never mind, I'll be fine."

"My friends are always more important than business, Sterling. Besides, everything is pretty much wrapped up here. Tomorrow is supposed to be a celebration brunch, but I can beg off."

He pulled back and stared up at her, ridiculously thankful for how easy she made everything. "What would the brunch have been if you hadn't bought them out?"

"Sad and awkward? Either way, I can get out of it. Peter will cover for me." She smoothed her hands gently over his head. Sterling pressed his head to her stomach again, hanging on tight. "We should probably go. We have a long drive ahead of us."

"I know, I just…"

"What?"

"Don't want to let go." He squeezed her impossibly tighter.

She leaned down to kiss his head. "I promise to hug you again later."

He pulled back again, now smiling in the way that made her heart flutter. "I think we can do better than a hug. You and I have some unfinished business, Albertine."

Alby blinked at him, unwilling to incriminate herself. She was no match for Sterling Thompson. He had never been without a girl in high school, and she doubted the intervening years changed anything. He was deadly handsome, had loads more experience, and had always been very good at the wooing portion of pursuit. He was the Prince Charming in every fairytale, and Alby was the goodhearted maid, not special enough or beautiful enough to be Cinderella. In stories, the Prince never ended up with the maid. He stood and leaned down to kiss her, an affectionate little gesture that, for unknown reasons, nearly brought tears to her eyes. At the moment, everything felt so impossible. Alby had never felt the disparity between them more.

Not satisfied to end on a kiss, he cupped her face in his hands and spoke. "Hey Alby." His voice was a soft whisper. His thumbs smoothed over her lips, sending shivers of delight from the back of her neck all the way to her ankles.

"Hmm." She peeled her eyes open and stared up at him, blinking in surprise by the depth of feeling she read there. One way or another, Sterling truly cared about her. She could see it in the tender set of his features.

"Thank you." Two little words, but they felt imbued with so much meaning, too much for Alby to parse through.

She swallowed hard, feeling confused and overwhelmed. Bess would know exactly what to say or do in this moment to gain the upper hand. She would offer a kiss or comment that would restore power. But Alby wasn't Bess. Not only did she have no idea what to say or do, she wasn't certain she wanted power. All she wanted was not to get hurt when things inevitably went awry between them. And they would, wouldn't they? She and Sterling weren't well suited to be together in any real way. Were they? But if not, what had those kisses been about?

"What?" Sterling asked. One of his hands now rested on her neck, his thumb smoothing up and down her windpipe. How did he instinctively know all the best ways to touch her? It was uncanny, as if someone had given him a roadmap of her body.

"Sterling." She paused and swallowed.

"Yes, Albertine?"

"Maybe you should be a masseuse."

One corner of his mouth tipped, flashing his devilish little dimple. A girl could get lost in that dimple. Alby knew, she'd seen it happen. "I don't think I could survive with a client list of one because," he leaned closer to whisper softly in her ear, "I don't want to be touching anyone but you."

She swallowed hard, grasping his forearm. "I pay really well."

He laughed, kissed her cheek, and took a step back. "Come on, let's get this dreaded event started before Duncan calls again." As he finished speaking, his phone rang once more. He was about to stuff it in his pocket when he caught sight of Alby's disapproving expression. Rolling his eyes, he answered the phone and spoke. "We'll be there soon, we're leaving in a minute." There was a pause and then he reached out and took her hand, giving it a squeeze. "Alby, she's coming with me." He disconnected without saying goodbye. "Duncan's glad you're coming, although there seems to be some confusion. He seems to think you're coming for him. Gonna have to find time to tell him you're all mine." He picked up her hand and kissed the back of it, tossing her a wink.

Yep, she was in definite trouble.

CHAPTER 20

"I had no idea it would take this long," Sterling mused. They packed up their things and drove a few hours, believing it would all be over by the time they got there. Now, three hours later, they were still waiting, sitting side by side in the uncomfortable hospital waiting room. Duncan emerged every hour or so with an update, looking anxious, exhausted, and ill at ease. He and Chelsea were strangers to each other, the pregnancy the result of a drunken hookup. Why either of them wanted him to be in the room was a mystery to Sterling.

"You should go," Sterling said, facing Alby and tucking a strand of hair behind her ear. She had to be exhausted, after her grueling weekend. But she smiled sweetly up at him, a hint of stubbornness in her expression.

"You go, I go, punk."

He smiled, resting his head on the wall to match her pose. "I'm a punk now?"

"You've always been a punk at heart."

"You're finally catching on," he said and because he couldn't resist any longer, leaned in to kiss her. It was supposed to be an innocent brush of lips, but she gave an adorable little sigh at the last minute and he slid his hand behind her neck, urging her closer as he deepened the kiss. They were alone in the room, or they were when the kiss started. Now someone cleared his throat, and it was a sound Sterling recognized. He rested his forehead on Alby's, not wanting to recognize what he might see in Duncan's face. He hadn't told Duncan about Alby, hadn't put a name to the new feelings now simmering inside him. He had wanted to keep them for himself, had been afraid Duncan might make light of something that felt far too precious for teasing or speculation.

"She's here," Duncan blurted, voice wobbly with tiredness and emotion.

Sterling straightened and blinked at him, feeling shocked for reasons he couldn't comprehend. Of course he knew Chelsea was pregnant. Of course he knew his lifelong friend was about to be a father. But now he actually was. Duncan Shepherd, immature idiot he sometimes was, was a dad. Alby nudged him lightly and he sprang up, reaching for Duncan and pulling him into a crushing hug. Duncan pressed his face to his shoulder and took a few shuddering breaths, trying to get himself back under control. "Congratulations," Sterling said, his voice wobbly, too. Childhood was really over; one of them was a father. He always secretly thought he would be the first to settle down and have a kid, but Duncan had beaten him to the punch. And now everything that came between them before this felt like silliness and fluff. Who cared if Duncan hooked up with Chelsea? She hadn't meant that much to Sterling, not nearly as much as… He turned to Alby, offering her a watery smile. She remained seated, uncertain of her place at the moment. He motioned her forward. She stood and shyly eased beside him.

Duncan, too overwhelmed to care who he hugged or why, turned his affection on her, swallowing her in an oversized hug that threatened to crush her. "Congratulations, Duncan," she whispered. "I can't wait to meet your little girl."

"She's beautiful and perfect," Duncan gushed and Sterling's throat sealed, cutting off his air.

"Of course she is," Alby agreed, beaming, eyes sparkling with unshed tears. Sterling slid his arm around her and she leaned into him. Duncan's eyes darted between them, but he was too over-whelmed with his own news to comment.

"They're going to get everything cleaned up and then you can hold her." His eyes settled on Sterling. "If you want to."

"Of course I want to. It's your little girl," Sterling choked. He was an uncle, ish.

"Will you call Birdie? She wanted me to let her know, but I…can't right now." He wrung his hands, looking suddenly miserable.

"Absolutely," Sterling agreed. His sister would want to know, of course. He wondered if the news would hurt her. Not for the first time, he was glad for Hayden Paxton and his presence in Birdie's life, and wasn't that a kick in the teeth.

Duncan wandered back out of the room, nodding dazedly. Sterling and Alby sank into a chair, his arm around her, her head on his chest. "I'm going to call Birdie," he announced unnecessarily as he pushed a button on his phone. Alby's only response was to nestle closer. His free hand smoothed up and down her arm. He both wished and didn't wish her to go. She had to be exhausted, and that made him feel bad. But he had no idea what he would do without her, how to face the current situation alone.

His sister's face flicked into view on his phone. Overseas cell rates being what they were, it was cheaper to do a video call on the inter-net. "Hey, what's up?" Birdie greeted him.

Sterling smiled, his heart turning over with a mixture of elation and longing. He missed his little sister with a persistent sort of ache, but he had never heard her sound so happy as she did since she went away. He had no idea if it was the job or the man. Maybe both.

"We're at the hospital. Duncan's a daddy."

She blinked at him. "Oh, wow. Is he there?"

"No, he left, but he wanted me to call you."

"Of course," she said, nodding a bit dazedly. "Tell him I said congratulations. I'll try to get hold of him later, when it's not so crazy. How are you doing?" She squinted and leaned closer, trying to read his face.

"I'm good. I mean I'm overwhelmed and exhausted, we've been here for hours waiting, but good, you know? It's exciting." He smiled so she would read the sincerity in his features. She smiled in response.

"I'm so glad," she said, sounding relieved, revealing her worry for him. "Is Mom there?"

"No."

"Who's 'we'? Whose head is in the picture?" She cocked her head trying to see. Beside him, Alby stiffened and tried to shrink away. He tipped the phone, including her in the frame, resting his head on hers.

"Albertine Mowry."

Beside Birdie, Hayden's head darted into the picture, eyebrows raised in surprise, mouth agape. His eyes flicked between Alby and Sterling and he grinned "Hey, Alby."

"Hi, Hayden," she said, sounding shy.

"It's good to see you," he said.

"You, too. How's Italy?" she asked, trying hard to pretend this was all normal and Sterling's sister wasn't staring at her in openmouthed shock.

"I can't complain at all," Hayden said, tossing her a little wink before he eased back out of the frame.

"That's…" Birdie stammered. "That's, uh, well, it's nice to see you again, Alby. Hi." She tucked her hair behind her ears, flustered and uncertain.

"Hi, Birdie. Congratulations on the job and, uh," her eyes darted to Hayden at the edge of the frame, "everything." In the background, Hayden snickered.

"Thank you. I hate to cut this short, but I have to go to work in a few minutes. But, um, Sterling, call me later, okay?" If it were possible, her eyes would be drilling holes through his forehead.

"Yes, ma'am," he said meekly. "Take care, Birdie. I love you."

"I love you, too, so much," Birdie said, blowing him a kiss.

"Later, Paxton," Sterling added.

"Back at you, Thompson," Hayden replied and the screen went black.

"You got me in trouble with my sister," Sterling declared.

"What did I do?" Alby asked, reaching up to smooth the hair at his temple. It wasn't sticking up, but her hand had a will of its own and needed to be there, apparently.

"You sat here looking all tempting and adorable, and now she has questions," he said, leaning in to nuzzle her cheek with his nose.

Get in line, Birdie, Alby thought. She had a few questions of her own. "She and Hayden seem happy."

"Blissfully so. It's gag-inducing," Sterling agreed.

"Liar, you're thrilled she's happy." He had moved on to nuzzling her ear and she was starting to lose the thread of the conversation. Her fingers sifted his hair and he took a nibble of her earlobe.

"True. But…"

"But what?" she asked and, oh no, did she gasp? Probably, if the way he smiled against her neck was any indication.

"But you have got to stop talking about my family members when I'm trying to incapacitate you. It's distracting."

"Should you be trying to incapacitate me in a hospital?" she asked.

"Where else? Plus, we're so very alone."

Someone cleared his throat behind them, proving the last statement untrue. "The baby's ready for viewing, if you can tear yourselves away," Duncan said dryly. Sterling had been prepared for his censure—Duncan hated to be kept out of the loop on any developments in his life. But the approval was a surprise, and a pleasant one. Or maybe it was relief. Maybe he was glad to know Sterling was well and truly over Chelsea and all that had passed between them.

"Y'all go on ahead," Alby shooed, waving her hand. "I don't want to intrude."

"You wouldn't begin to know how," Sterling said, clasping her hand and hauling her up beside him. "This is momentous, we should all be there."

Alby glanced at Duncan, awaiting his input. He reached forward and put his arm around her shoulders, giving them a squeeze. "I've known you as long as I've known Sterling, Alby. Of course I want you there."

She walked between the two tall men through the maze of hallways. Duncan pushed open a hospital door, stood aside, and awkwardness descended. The woman in the bed, presumably Chelsea, looked at Sterling like every woman in Alby's memory looked at Sterling, as if he were her every dream come true. Was that how she looked at him? With such hopefulness and adulation, as if he were her personal knight in shining armor? *I hope not,* she thought. She never wanted to be one more person on the list of people Sterling had to rescue.

"Sterling," Chelsea breathed.

"Hi, Chelsea," Sterling said. His voice sounded tense, strained, his eyes focused with laser precision on the squirming bundle in Chelsea's grasp. His hand edged to Alby's and held on tight. Chelsea noted the action, blinking rapidly.

"Who's this?" she asked, giving Alby a full body scan.

"This is our friend, Alby," Duncan said. He eased forward and peered at the baby as if convincing himself she was real and still there. Chelsea bounced the baby, her gaze never leaving Alby.

"My girlfriend," Sterling added, and Alby and Chelsea seemed to share the same shocked flinch.

Apparently we're continuing the delusion, Alby thought. But, she reasoned, Sterling needed the façade at the moment. It couldn't be easy to be faced with his recently ex-girlfriend and the baby she had with his best friend. Even if Duncan and Chelsea weren't together, it wasn't an easy or fun situation. She gave his hand an encouraging squeeze. He returned it, tossing her a smile.

"Congratulations," Sterling added, tugging Alby forward as they approached the bed.

"Thanks," Chelsea said, voice hoarse with strain. She offered the baby to Duncan without taking her eyes off Sterling. Smiling, Duncan drew the baby close, staring at her in wonder a moment before passing her off to Sterling.

"Meet your Uncle Sterling," he whispered.

Sterling let go of Alby's hand to cuddle the baby close, tipping her slightly so Alby could catch a view. She gasped.

"Oh, my goodness, she's gorgeous," Alby whispered.

"I know," Duncan said, beaming. Behind him, Chelsea remained quiet and watchful.

"How long has this been going on?" Chelsea demanded.

Sterling seemed unable to answer, too deep in newborn adoration. Alby was enjoying watching him watch the baby, but clearly someone had to answer.

"It's relatively new," she said.

"When did you meet?" Chelsea said. The overt suspicion in her tone told everyone she was ready to do the math, to make certain Sterling hadn't cheated on her while she cheated on him.

"Kindergarten," Alby said. "We reconnected last month."

"But I thought…" Chelsea began and trailed away. She was exhausted, both emotionally and physically drained. Alby didn't think it was a good time to discuss anything, but it was clear to everyone she needed some sort of explanation or closure. "I thought you and I were working through things."

Sterling's head came up, staring at her unblinking. Alby could feel his tension, anger, and indignation, could practically hear his thoughts. *I'm standing here holding the baby she had with another man, and she thinks we're getting back together?* He was right to be incensed. On the other hand, the girl was at her lowest point. Sterling took a deep breath and glanced down at the baby in his hands before speaking.

"Chelsea, I'm not certain we would have worked, even if nothing had happened between you and Duncan. We had issues, serious issues, that showed no hope of working out." He let out a breath and the tension eased from his body. "I'm not angry at you anymore. I'm done with that. I want you to be well and happy, truly. This baby is a blessing, and I hope you enjoy her. But you and I are over completely, with no hope of ever reconnecting again. Even if Alby and I weren't together, you and I wouldn't be. It's over."

She started to cry, great heaving sobs, and the awkwardness ratcheted up even more because no one wanted to be the one to comfort her. Duncan seemed annoyed by her tears, Sterling was uncomfortable, and Alby's overblown sense of compassion squirmed in sympathy. *She* wanted to go forward and hug the poor girl, and how awkward would that be?

"We should go," Sterling said gently. "Congratulations to you both. She's amazing." He handed the baby back to Duncan, took Alby's hand, and led her out of the room.

CHAPTER 21

It was a sleepy, silent walk back to Sterling's car. He opened the passenger door for Alby and waited to close it until she was safely tucked inside. She waited to speak until he was buckled and on the roadway.

"Are you doing okay?"

"I really am," he said, turning to her with a smile. "Thank you for making me do that, it was the closure I've been looking for all these months." He let out a breath, more tension draining from his shoulders.

Alby faced forward, thinking through the night's events. Even after giving birth Chelsea looked like Sterling's usual type, beautiful and put together. Meanwhile Alby felt every one of the twenty-six hours she had now been awake. If someone lined them side by side, she would likely be mistaken for the one who'd recently been in labor. *It's an illusion,* she reminded herself. Their pretend relationship had served her function at her work weekend, and now it had served Sterling's function during his difficult encounter with his ex. They were friends, only friends, and she didn't need to be a beauty queen for that.

"Are you hungry?" Sterling asked, reaching over to give her leg a gentle squeeze.

"Honestly I think I'm too tired for hunger, but you must be starved. Stop and pick something up, if you like," Alby said.

He steered into an all night fast food establishment. "You should get something. I bet you'll be hungry once you smell food."

"You're probably right. I'll take a cheeseburger."

He quirked an eyebrow at her. "Just one?"

"Some of us do not eat like we're still high school quarterbacks."

"You're so tiny. It makes me anxious you're not getting enough," he said.

She tried not to frown. "You're so tiny," wasn't exactly the dream compliment women wanted to hear from an attractive male. *We're friends, only friends.* "A cheeseburger is plenty, thank you."

He ordered and scooted forward to wait their turn in line. "Hey, Alby, I'm starting to sound like a broken record here, but thank you. Thank you so much for everything you're doing on my behalf."

"I don't feel like I'm doing anything."

"That's because you're you, so being you doesn't feel like extra effort, but you dropped everything to be here for me during a difficult time, gave me a job when I needed one most, forgave me when I was incandescently stupid." He leaned forward and cupped her jaw in his hand, lowering his tone to an intimate whisper. "Plus, girl, you can kiss like nobody's business."

She probably looked like a trapped bird, because that was how she felt, but the car behind them beeped, urging them forward. Sterling dropped his hand and put the car into gear, arriving at the window for their food.

For a while the silence was taken up with food. Alby mindlessly chewed her cheeseburger, not really tasting it. She wasn't hungry, but she did feel a bit weak. Maybe her sugar was low. In any case, the burger helped her feel a bit more stable. She took a deep breath, clearing her cluttered mind. This was Sterling. They were pals, nothing more. She rested her hand on his arm. "Are you okay to drive? You must be exhausted."

"I'm fine." He tossed her a smile. "You look all done in. Just rest, I'll get you home in one piece."

"I know you will," she said softly, nestling into the seat. She didn't mean to fall asleep, but the next thing she knew, Sterling was whispering her name.

"Alby."

Her eyes popped open. She was no longer in his car. Instead she was snuggled firmly in his arms, held aloft under the eaves of her porch. "We're home?"

"Yes. I was going to carry you up to your room, in a full-on romantic hero maneuver, but I don't know how to open your door. Sorry."

"S'okay," she said groggily, sliding down his chest as he set her down. She entered the code to open her door. Sterling disappeared and reappeared a second later with her luggage. She turned to thank him, but he bypassed her and headed toward her room, giving her the odd experience of trundling behind him to her bedroom. Once there, he set her case in the middle of the room and looked around, as if seeing it anew, even though he'd been there on the night of the party. Alby caught sight of the clock, nearly four AM.

"You should stay over," she said. She hated the thought of him driving home, and her efficient housekeeper, Berta, always kept the guest room freshly prepared, even though Alby hadn't had an overnight guest in ages.

"It's adorable how you think I had any other notion," Sterling said. She watched in rapt amazement as he yanked his shirt over his head, slipped off his shoes, and shucked out of his pants until, quicker than she would have thought possible, he stood before her in his boxers. She stared at him in unblinking fascination, as if he were paid entertainment, remaining stock still while he peeled back her bedspread and climbed between the sheets.

"Okay, I'm going to nip into the bathroom for a quick shower because," she waved a hand at her face.

"Sure," he said, smiling up at her, his tone radiating supreme confidence.

"Okay," she repeated. She pivoted on one foot, strode into the bathroom, closed the door and leaned on it, mouthing, *Oh, my word.* Sterling Thompson was in her bed. In his underpants. She pulled out her phone, desperate to text somebody, anybody who could tell her what to do. Bess was the only person who could possibly give her any direction in this scenario, but it was four in the morning. Why wasn't there some sort of emergency hotline for this sort of thing? A helpline for inexperienced virgins who inadvertently wound up with a hot guy in their beds. In his underpants.

She bent over and sucked oxygen. *It's only Sterling,* she reminded herself. *You've seen him in his skivvies before, lots of times.* The high school football team had gloried in walking around in as little as possible when she was their manager, and sometimes in nothing at all. She had seen all of them in their underwear and a handful naked. It had been quite the education back then, something she hadn't told her overtly conservative parents about, for fear they would make her quit.

Remembering high school helped her breathing return to normal. Things like this weren't a big deal to Sterling, didn't mean the same to him as they did to her. How many times had their group of friends gone skinny-dipping back in the day? Too many too count. Not Alby, of course. She had always remained sitting on the bank to "watch their clothes," in case someone came along and stole them. Or at least that had been her pathetic excuse. In reality she had never been as carefree and easy with her body as everyone else. Now that she thought of it, no one had seen her naked since she was a baby. Even at her annual doctor appointment, she was always careful to clutch the paper gown tight and huddle under the paper blanket.

She turned on the shower and washed quickly, clinging to her rational nature for comfort. Sterling did not mean anything at all by his current state of undress, even if it was taking place in her bed. He was and had always been comfortable with his body, and why shouldn't he be? The man looked like a living sculpture, a perfect specimen of masculinity, tight muscle and bronzed skin. That was absolutely all this was. And he knew Alby was likewise inexperienced and innocent. They were friends, pals who went back a long way, all the way to kindergarten. And it wasn't as if they didn't have precedent. Already this week she had slept in his embrace, fully clothed and on top of the covers, but still. There was precedent. She would not make a big deal of this.

She combed her hair, brushed her teeth, and slid into an innocuous sleeping outfit, shorts and a t-shirt. *Bess made you buy new lingerie,* her traitorous mind suddenly recalled. *Shut up and take a seat, crazytown.* That was all she needed, to emerge from the bathroom wearing a silk nightie. Sterling would think she misconstrued things, might think she was tossing herself at him. As if she'd have any idea what to do after that. She hadn't kissed anyone since Hogue when she was seventeen years old. *Sad, so sad.* When this was over, she needed to have a date, a real one. Maybe Sterling could help her find someone and coach her on what to do. Maybe it would require hands on instruction and he…

She pressed her palms to her flaming cheeks. *Go to bed, Alby,* she commanded herself. With a bracing breath, she opened the door and stepped into the bedroom. Sterling was still and silent. *Probably already asleep,* she thought. He had to be as exhausted as she was, maybe more so because he hadn't napped in the car.

She strode across the room and slid into bed, staring up at the dark ceiling, her hands clutching the blanket like a lifeline. *I'm lying next to Sterling Thompson. In his underpants. But it's fine because this is what friends do. I guess?* She had no frame of reference for her current situation, but then she never did. Most of the time she felt like she was on the outside of everything, looking in. Until the last few weeks with Sterling when she'd begun to feel a part of things, an active participant in her life, someone who had some understanding of what was going on. She'd begun to feel a hopeful sort of expectancy about the future. *This is how it feels to be alive.* Maybe with his tutelage she could continue to grow, to experience new things. *Like sleeping next to a boy. In his underpants.*

"What's the matter?" Sterling asked, startling her.

"Nothing, why?"

"You're all tensed up." He rolled toward her, resting his face on his open hand.

"It was a busy weekend. It takes me a while to process everything," she said, the truth. Her mind felt like it was whirling a thousand miles an hour, spitting out images she had no hope of sorting. Hart. Whitney. Peter. Duncan. Chelsea. The baby. Sterling, Sterling again. Sterling kissing her. Sterling in his underpants. She was glad for the darkness to cover her blush.

"C'mere," Sterling said, reaching for her. He pulled her against him and rolled her on her side facing away from him, spooning her from behind. He smoothed his hand over her hair a few times. "Your bed smells just like you. So good." He placed a little kiss behind her earlobe. A few seconds later, he was asleep.

Alby listened to his deep, steady breathing, the comforting warmth from his body radiating around her, seeping through her. *There is absolutely no way I'll be able to sleep like this,* was her last coherent thought until morning.

CHAPTER 22

*A*few hours later, Alby woke alone. *See?* She chided herself. *He merely needed a place to crash. You should not make such a big deal of everything.* In Sterling's world, boys and girls could apparently have sleepovers and it meant absolutely nothing. It wasn't likely they would find themselves out that late together again, so it wasn't something that would likely recur. Sterling would not sleep over again. She would not feel the secure weight of his arm over her waist while he lay beside her. In his underpants. Whew. What a relief. A relief, not a disappointment. That odd ache in her chest was probably hunger. She should eat something, get her blood sugar back up to its proper setting after the last few mixed up days.

She brushed her teeth, piled her hair up out of the way, and strode to the kitchen, stopping short at the sound of pots and pans being moved about. *It's Berta's day off,* she remembered. Who was in her kitchen and why?

Stealthily, hugging the wall, she stole closer and poked her head around for a glance.

"I see you, Albertine," Sterling said easily, flipping an omelet with the same deftness and dexterity he did everything else.

She eased further into the kitchen, blinking like Bambi in a sunlit meadow. Fully dressed now, Sterling had commandeered complete control of her kitchen.

"Hungry?" he asked, when she remained mutely rooted to the spot.

"Yes?"

He tossed her one of his devastating smiles. "Not sure?"

"No?"

He chuckled. "You wake up befuddled." He gazed at her over the top of the island that separated them. "Cute, but befuddled."

"Thank you?"

"Can you grab a couple of plates, please?"

"Yes?" When she still made no move to leave her new favorite spot, Sterling spoke again.

"Need some help?"

"No?" He was fully dressed and, by the wet curl of his hair, apparently showered, but Alby couldn't stop picturing the entire scene with him still in his boxers. Which would totally not be appropriate, not to mention a burn risk for him. All that exposed skin... "Plates," she declared, heading toward the cupboard with determination. She reached for them, Sterling's eyes warming the back of her. Keeping her own eyes downcast, she set the plates on the island beside him and turned to go. He tugged her back, resting his free arm companionably over her shoulders.

"I didn't know what you like in an omelet, so I made it the way I like mine," he said.

"I'm not picky," she replied, trying hard not to sniff him. He had undoubtedly used her shower gel, but it smelled different on him than it did on her, cleaner and more masculine. How does a man make freesia smell masculine?

"Good news for me. What are you thinking about? You look confused."

"I was wondering if testosterone changes the smell of things," she said.

"Ah," he said, nodding as if it had been a normal thing to say, as if anything was normal about this whole experience. Maybe for him it was. Maybe he routinely woke in a strange woman's house and made breakfast.

"Do you do this often?" she motioned to the omelets.

"Lately, yes."

Her heart sank until he continued. "Since Birdie left, I've been trying to cook more, to give my mom a break. She works long hours, and the last thing she needs when she comes home is to cook."

"Oh," she said, heart melting now. Few things were more endearing than a guy who took good care of his mom.

He plated the omelets and picked them up, nodding his head in the direction of the breakfast nook. Alby followed in his wake, still feeling a bit dazed. No one but her housekeeper or mother had ever made food for her. She sat, belatedly realizing she should have done something more to help when Sterling retrieved the coffee and the juice.

"I'm sorry, I'm such a dolt. I should have gotten that," Alby said.

"No, you should remain seated while I take care of you for once," Sterling said with warmhearted sincerity. "It's a privilege to take care of the woman who takes care of everyone else."

Her cheeks warmed. "How can you be this sweet on so little sleep?"

"I learned from the master," he said, tossing her a wink.

It was a patented Sterling Thompson gesture, that wink, and it brought her back to reality. He was used to this sort of thing, had likely done it a million times before for a million different women. There was absolutely nothing special about Alby or this experience. Far from making her sad, she felt relieved. They were friends, no biggie. Smiling now, she picked up her fork and tucked into the omelet, which was every bit as delicious as she guessed it would be.

"Why is it physically impossible for you to be bad at things?" she demanded.

"Let's compare finances and you can ask me again," he said.

She laughed. "I'd like to remind you I'm an heiress."

"An heiress who is a millionaire," he said, and she froze. He glanced up, noting her lack of movement. "I was joking, Alby. I don't actually care that you're a millionaire. You know that."

She swallowed hard and dabbed her lips with the napkin. "That's good because I, uh, have a little confession." She cleared her throat and stared hard at a spot to the left of his head. "I'm not a millionaire. I'm, um, actually a billionaire."

He blinked at her. "You're joking. Right?"

She shook her head. "My dad invented a product that is used in every state, for every paved road. We get a percentage every time someone paves with asphalt. It's a tiny percentage, much less than one percent. But it happens thousands of times every single day, for the last forty years." It was a secret no one else knew, not even Peter. The royalty was separate from the business; it went into her personal account, an inheritance from her father. She worked because it gave her purpose and she cared about her employees, not because she needed the money to stay solvent.

Now Sterling was frozen, staring at her like she was a freak. This was why she didn't tell people, because of the expression on his face. He stuffed a bite of omelet between his lips and chewed thoughtfully. "I suppose it doesn't change anything from my perspective," he said after he finally swallowed. "My wealth is as close to a million dollars as it will ever be to a billion."

She let out a breath she didn't know she'd been holding. "I've never told anyone before."

"Tell me all your secrets, girl." She had petered out on her omelet, only able to eat two thirds of it. He reached across the table and slid the remainder onto his plate.

"Are you going to tell me yours?" she asked.

"You already know them," he said, shooting her a brilliant smile that looked so happy and lighthearted. She smiled in response. A flicker of tension sprang up between them. Sterling ate his last bite and pushed his plate away. Before she could find out what he might do next, his phone rang. "My mom," he said, his tone an apology. Alby smiled and stood to clear their plates, but when she passed by him, he snagged her around the waist and pulled her into his lap, tipping the phone from his ear to kiss her cheek. "It's probably the softener, Mom. Did you check the salt? You lift the lid and look in, the salt should be over the…right, okay. I'll pick some up on my way home.

Was there anything else?" He listened a few beats, nodding. "Right, okay. I'll call him."

The call finished. He set his phone aside and pressed his face to her shoulder, inhaling. "Everything okay?" Alby asked, smoothing her hand along his forearm.

"Same old, same old. My mom has a lot of questions about house stuff, and car stuff, and financial stuff. And she said my dad left her some bizarre messages in the middle of the night."

She turned to face him, unconsciously nestling closer in a bid to get more comfortable. He slid both arms around her and pulled her tighter. "What does that mean?"

"Usually that he's bottoming out into one of his depressive phases."

"Is there anything I can do to help?" she asked, her palm skimming over his cheek. She hated to see him so sad when only a few minutes ago he had seemed so lighthearted.

"This," he said, giving her a squeeze. "And maybe a bit of this." He unclasped his hands and used one of them to tip her face, leaning forward to kiss her. She could tell it was probably meant to be a soft and gentle kiss. The effect was ruined when Alby responded to him like a gasoline soaked newspaper to flame, twisting to face him, circling his neck with her arms, and leaning into the kiss like a drowning victim in search of oxygen. She would have been mortified, except Sterling responded to her response, his hands easing to her hips, urging her impossibly closer, his kiss suddenly more urgent. Her fingers stabbed into his ridiculously thick hair—could the man not even go bald like normal people? She had no idea what might have become of them, but at that moment his phone started to ring with renewed urgency, freezing them, making them both aware of their actions.

"It's my dad," he whispered, lips moving against hers. "I should…I should get that. Right?"

She smiled, her lips pulling his into a smile, too. "Yes. Be dutiful."

"Dutiful," he muttered, amused. He pulled away to answer. Alby eased off his lap and continued clearing the dishes, keeping her distance at the far side of the room. Eavesdropping on Sterling worked to keep her mind off that kiss. He sounded almost pleading with his father, trying to reason away his dad's dark mood. At last he hung up and let out a breath.

She faced him. "Okay?"

"It is what it is." He sighed and forced a smile. "What do you have going on today?"

She had an entire list of things that required her attention, both for her job and for charity. But she sensed Sterling needed a friend, needed *her*. "Not a thing. How about you?"

His smile became more genuine. "You want to come to my store with me?"

CHAPTER 23

Sterling's enthusiasm for his bookstore was boyish and endearing. Holding tight to Alby's hand, he led her over every inch of it, from front to back and to the front again. She allowed him to prattle, waiting to speak until he was finished.

"I love this personalized tour, but you know I've been in here before," she said.

His jaw dropped. "What? No. When?"

"Every Thursday for the last six years," she said.

He blinked at her, horrified. Alby had been coming into his store weekly for the last six years? How blind had he been to her? She reached out to toy with one of the buttons on his shirt, one corner of her mouth tipping. "Got ya."

He erased the distance between them and picked her up. "Now I'm going to have to think of a way to punish you."

"Horrors," she said, belatedly realizing it was probably not the correct thing to say when a gorgeous man held you in his arms.

Sterling didn't seem to mind. He brushed his nose on hers. "Have you ever really been in here before?"

"Yes. A few months ago when I heard what happened between you and Duncan. I came to see you, but you weren't here. Your mom was working the store. We had a nice chat."

Unbidden, his arms tightened on her waist. He knew exactly the time she referenced because he'd been in the psychiatric ward of the hospital on a voluntary commit. "Did she mention where I was?"

She shook her head. "She seemed glad to talk about anything but you. We talked about spring bulbs."

"Spring bulbs?" he repeated, smiling now.

"Daffodils and tulips. Believe it or not, Sterling Thompson, you were not always the sole focus of my thoughts and attention."

"How about now?" he asked, holding her impossibly tighter, lips brushing over hers.

"I'm hardly thinking of daffodils at all, tulips maybe a little," she replied, tilting her head slightly to allow him easier access.

"Did you say tulips or two lips?" he asked, his lips working against hers.

"We're going to have to borrow Duncan's baby so we can make that an official dad joke."

Laughing, he gave her a peck and set her down.

"Have you talked to him today?" she asked.

"No."

She tossed him a look. He sighed. "You're really going to make me a better person in all the ways, aren't you? I promise to call and check on him, see if he needs anything. Better?"

"You would have done the right thing with or without my urging," she said.

"Probably later rather than sooner. You do make me want to be a better man, Alby." He tipped his head, as if struck anew over the truth of his statement.

She surprised them both by easing her arms around him. "But, Sterling, how would that be possible when you're already one of the best men I know?"

He cupped her face. "Did I show you the break room? It's spectacular, so very private and hidden." His thumb smoothed over her lips. She stood on her toes and his phone rang. They froze.

"Your mom?" she guessed.

"My dad." Sighing he eased away and reached for his phone. It stopped ringing before he could answer. "I guess I should call him back."

"Why don't we go over there in person? We can take him some food from the diner."

"I can't ask you to do that," he said.

"You didn't," she reminded him. "Come on." She reached for his hand, giving him a tug toward the door. They stopped at the diner, picked up food for all three of them, and headed toward his dad's house. Sterling led the way to the door but paused on the step, facing her.

"This might not be pretty, Alby. My dad...he can get kind of low, sometimes says harsh things. He, well, he wallows."

"Sterling, I've been aware of your dad's condition since before I understood what mental illness was. I am fine. Please do not worry about me. I'm here to support you." Smiling, she rested her hand on his forearm. Sterling blinked at her, staring hard. It was impossible not to contrast her with every other woman he'd dated. He'd hardly introduced any of them to his father, and when he had, it hadn't gone well. Chelsea in particular had a hard time with it, decrying any time spent with his dad, citing her discomfort as an excuse. But Alby, he knew, was sincere in her desire to help. And having her there beside him made all the difference. It was like having Birdie, but better because he'd always had to run interference between his dad and Birdie. There wouldn't be that need with Alby. She was there solely for him, his support system. His relief at her presence was immense.

"Girl, you make me swoon," he said, tipping forward to brush his lips on hers, smiling all the while.

His father answered his knock on the fifth try, looking disheveled and greasy. A stale smell eked out of his house. "Hey, Dad, we brought food."

His father gripped the door, squinting at the outside light. "Who's we? Is your mother here?"

"No, it's Albertine Mowry," Sterling said, motioning to her with his free hand.

His father blinked at Alby, trying to focus. "The Mowry girl? What's she doing here?"

"Alby's my girlfriend," Sterling declared and Alby blinked at the ease with which he lied to his father. Clearly he needed the continued delusion to make it through the evening. Mr. Thompson's eyes narrowed on her. She smiled hard, touching her head affectionately to Sterling's shoulder, playing her part. "So, anyway, we brought food."

His dad blinked and finally moved aside with a heavy sigh. "Well, come in, I guess." They followed him to his kitchen. It wasn't a hovel, but there were signs of recent neglect. He sank to the table with another sigh as Sterling set the food on the table. Unbidden, Alby guessed at which cupboard contained glasses and set about pouring drinks for each of them.

"Thank you, sweetheart," Sterling said, tossing her a smile as she handed him his drink.

"How long has this been going on?" his father demanded, eyes darting between them.

"Not long," Sterling said. He sat and patted the spot beside him, urging Alby to do the same. She sat, trying hard to ignore the messy kitchen. She was a worker bee by nature, more comfortable doing things than sitting still, especially if she thought she could be of help. Cleaning the kitchen would no doubt be satisfying, but Sterling clearly needed her emotional support more than his father needed a clean kitchen. Angling her chair slightly to block the view, she instead picked up her fork and started to eat.

"I was sure sorry to hear about your parents, Alby," his father said. "Gone too soon, gone too soon."

"Thank you, sir. I couldn't agree more. I miss them every day."

"Good people," his father said.

"Yes, sir," she agreed.

He tipped his head at her. "Aren't you Sterling's boss now?"

She smiled. "Yes, sir."

"And that doesn't bother you?" he prodded.

She chuckled. "No, sir. I suppose because I don't think of him as my employee. I think of him as that boy I've known since we were five." She frowned, once again reminded of the old disparity between them.

"You two do go back a ways," he said, brightening. "I don't know that I could have stood being with a woman who made more than me, though. Takes a lot of fortitude." Now his gaze turned to Sterling, studying him as if wondering how much fortitude he possessed. It made Alby want to defend him.

"Sterling is nothing if not secure, Mr. Thompson. He's a man who knows where he stands in the world. And money is not his main concern, thankfully. We're good friends who have a lot of fun together. For now, that seems like enough."

"Preach, girl," Sterling said, reaching over to squeeze her knee, which made her jump.

"Why you got to tickle me when I'm trying to do you right?" she complained.

"Because I can't resist when you look so cute," he murmured, leaning forward to kiss the tip of her nose.

"Have you talked to your sister?" his dad asked.

"Yesterday, in fact. I called to tell her Duncan had his baby. A girl, she's cute. You'll meet her eventually, I'm sure," Sterling said.

"She still with that Paxton boy?"

"To the best of my knowledge, yes," Sterling said.

"He's gonna break her heart," her father said sadly. "Birdie's too soft for a boy like that."

"Birdie's stronger than you give her credit for, she'll be fine. And he seems pretty crazy about her," Sterling said.

"For now," his dad said. He was a pessimist on the best of days. In his downward spiral, pessimism was a step up. The weight of constantly trying to pull him up was exhausting and draining.

"Mr. Thompson, I remember you being quite the singer," Alby said. Sterling looked at her like she was crazy, but his father actually smiled.

"I don't know what you're talking about," he said, sounding coy.

"Come on now," she said, giving him a conspiratorial smile. "I sat by you at a few too many games. I know you can belt the national anthem with the best of them."

His dad shrugged, looking pleased as punch. Sterling swung his amazed gaze from Alby to his father. "Is that true, Dad? Can you sing?"

"A real man has no need to brag, Sterling, but yes, I'm an amazing singer."

The three of them laughed together. It didn't take too much coaxing from Alby and Sterling before the older man stood in the center of the kitchen, belting the National Anthem, hand on heart. When he finished, they gave him a standing ovation. He bowed, smiling, and the rest of the night ended on a high note.

Sterling drove Alby home in silence, shaking his head the whole way.

"What?" she asked.

"You. You're just...you're so magical, Alby."

"What was in your tea tonight, Sterling?" she teased.

"A big dose of reality," he said.

He walked her to her door and they faced off. "So, back to work tomorrow."

"That's the same rumor I hear," she said, resting her shoulder against the bricks. He followed suit and picked up one of her hands.

"Are you nervous?"

"Why would I be nervous?" she asked.

He pointed between them. "The big debut. Everyone who went on the trip is going to blab, if they haven't already."

"Oh." Alby hadn't thought of that. Tomorrow everyone would be talking about her and Sterling and their fake relationship. How was she going to look when it ended? Like a fool? Heartbroken? Neither of those was a good option.

"You're squinting at me," he accused, smoothing his finger between her brows.

"I'm not certain I thought through all the ramifications of this venture."

Far from being offended, he grinned at her. "That's CEO talk. Come down to my level."

"How do I do that?"

"I'm so glad you asked," he said, stepping forward to kiss her breathless. She stood on her toes and leaned into him, once again practically pouncing on him in her haste. She was probably coming off desperate in her wholehearted response to him, but she couldn't seem to help it. Being kissed by Sterling was like nothing else, a sensory explosion that left her boneless and brainless. Worse, it would likely end at any moment. Once they decided on a graceful exit for their fake relationship, she'd be back to square one—alone and untouched, quite literally.

"No one has touched me since my parents died," she blurted, wincing at her stupidity. Inexperienced as she was, she still knew men didn't like sad statements of blatant need.

Sterling blinked at her, his thumb tracing a gentle path around her ear. "Then I guess we have a lot of time to make up for," he said softly. He kissed her forehead and slid his arms around her, easing her into an affectionate hug. She returned the favor, resting her head on his heart.

"Do you want to come in?" she offered, her brain immediately conjuring the image of him in the middle of her room, once again stripping to his boxers. She squeezed her eyes closed. *Get it together, you forsaken pervert.*

"I would love to," Sterling said, sounding regretful. His hand rubbed an enticing little circle on her lower back that had the same boneless result as his kisses. Alby clutched his shirt, using it as a prop to keep herself aloft. "But my mom is having a problem with the water softener and needs me to take a look."

She eased away to look up at him. "If you take care of your mom and dad, who takes care of you?"

His mouth opened, but no sound came out for a few beats, as if the question had caught him by surprise. "I think maybe you do," he said at last, softly, wonderingly.

"Thank goodness," Alby said, and this time she was the instigator, standing on her toes to kiss him with purpose, bestowing care and affection. And now Sterling was the one to respond with unbridled enthusiasm, picking her up and pressing her into the wall until his phone buzzed. He pulled away, resting his forehead on hers, his breathing hard and unsteady.

"So anyway, I'll see you tomorrow," he said, trying and failing for nonchalance.

"Yes, very good, Mr. Thompson. Excellent job this weekend, by the way."

He smiled and kissed her cheek. "Best boss ever." He waited to make sure she made it safely inside. Alby waved goodbye and then dodged to the window to watch him drive away, smiling like a lunatic until he was far out of sight.

CHAPTER 24

Sterling didn't see Alby for four days, but not for lack of trying on both their parts. On her end, the merger plus her absence created a tsunami of work. Plus Hart had arrived to tag along with Alby and try to smooth the merger process. The legal paperwork, transfer of money, and logistics wouldn't take place for several weeks. But the ball was rolling now and Alby was unbelievably busy.

Likewise in the evenings, Sterling was busy with personal matters. His dad was nearing the bottom of one of his cycles and required almost nightly consolation and cajoling. Sterling brought him food and attempted to coax him out of his depressive stupor. He even tried talking to him about medication, but his dad wouldn't hear of it. Looked at him, in fact, as if Sterling were the one who was sick.

"What are you talking about? I'm not going to the doctor. I just need something good to come along," his dad insisted. One night out of desperation he called Birdie, but that only made things worse as his dad listed all the ways Birdie could end up dead during her Mediterranean adventure. Finally it was Paxton who found a graceful exit for them, and Sterling was thankful. He wished he had someone to bail him out and thought wistfully of Alby, somehow knowing she would likely handle his dad as well as she had handled him the other night.

His mother's water softener was kaput. He spent a full evening installing a new one, Taylor holding a light for him and probing him about Alby.

"If you're really together, why aren't you with her right now?" Taylor, ever suspicious of the new arrangement, asked for the third time.

"I don't know, Taylor. I thought it would be so much more fun to lie on the concrete installing this softener while you yammer in my ear and shine a light in my face," Sterling said, annoyed. In truth the space and time away from Alby was making him cranky. And Hart Wentworth was everywhere lately, her constant shadow.

And then there was Duncan who, to everyone's surprise, was splitting parenting duties with Chelsea in full, taking the baby for half the week. Except he had no idea what he was doing and called Sterling in a panic. Sterling, in turn, brought his mother along. The two of them showed up at Duncan's door to help. His mother spent a few hours showing him the ropes of proper newborn care while Sterling washed his dishes and cleaned out his fridge, something the usually immaculate Duncan had never needed help with before. And then, for a solid hour while Duncan slept, Sterling held the baby and stared at her, marveling over every tiny feature like the love-addled baby addict he was now. And he realized he was once again jealous of Duncan. Not because of Chelsea, but because he had this tiny bundle of perfection in his life, making everything else feel insignificant. *Oh, sweet mercy, I have baby fever,* Sterling thought, but he couldn't seem to muster much chagrin over the realization. He was almost thirty years old. It was time to put aside childish things and settle down.

Tomorrow. I am going to connect with Alby if it kills me. While the baby slept on, he plotted his course.

The next morning he had a meeting with Alby and the other project managers. She entered the room wearing one of the new dresses Bess helped her pick, and Sterling's breath caught. He sent her a surreptitious text before the meeting began.

. . .

HOT GIRL ALERT.

SHE READ the text and looked around, eyes narrowed in confusion. He sighed and she glanced at him. He pointed to her. Finally realizing his meaning, her cheeks flushed a rosy shade of pink. And then Hart Wentworth entered and took note of her flush, his expression a mirror of Sterling's. Something within Sterling tightened in response, and he worked to push it away. *I will not be jealous of Hart. Alby is not interested in him, hasn't even glanced at him.*

Hart must have felt the heat from his glare because he looked up and locked eyes with Sterling, silent communication passing between them.

Mine, Sterling silently declared.

We'll see, Hart silently replied, then leaned close and whispered something to Alby that made her laugh.

Somehow in the intervening days since their return from Atlanta, Sterling had made nice with Alby's secretary, Sandra. Older women had always liked him, and it bugged him to no end that Sandra didn't. Maybe it was because he put forth so much extra effort to woo her, or maybe she was happy to see Alby with someone. Whatever the reason, when he showed up at her desk before noon and presented her with her favorite nonfat latte, she smiled and waved him into Alby's office without her usual hesitation or inquisition.

Sterling set his basket of supplies on the table and got to work setting them up. In need of some water, he slipped into the bathroom, but before he could turn it on, the outer door opened. He eased to the opening of the bathroom, ready to startle Alby who would no doubt be in work mode. Instead he observed her cousin Peter, stealthy and silent as he rifled Alby's desk and woke up her computer. Quietly, Sterling took out his phone and recorded him. After enough time had passed to make it clear what Peter was doing, he lowered his phone slightly and spoke.

"Looking for something?"

Peter froze, caught, guilty. He realized it was only Sterling and plastered a sneer back over his face. "Oh, it's you. Aladdin."

Sterling smiled, but it likely wasn't a friendly expression. "If I'm Aladdin, I guess that makes you Jafar."

Before he could respond, the outer door opened and Alby tripped in, followed by Hart. They were in their own conversation, laughing together, so it took them a few beats to notice the tension in the room. Alby came to a sudden halt. "Peter." Then, eyeing him, "Sterling. Did I know you were coming?"

"No, I scheduled a lunch appointment with Sandra, thought I would surprise you. Instead I surprised your cousin here."

All eyes returned to Peter. "What's going on?" Alby asked.

"I was looking for something," Peter said.

"What?" Alby asked, tone turning sharper.

Peter and Hart looked at each other, silent communication passing between them. Sterling tensed. Whatever this was, it wouldn't be good. Peter straightened and smoothed his already perfect lapels. "I'm sorry to have to do it like this, Alby, but Sterling is not who you think he is. He's been stealing from you, and Hart I can prove it."

"Wha…" Sterling began, indignant, but Alby held up a hand, halting him. She turned her steady, questioning gaze on Hart. He looked at Sterling, looked at her, and took a deep breath.

"My first day here, Peter approached me with a plan to out you and combine forces as co-CEO's. Step one was to frame Sterling for embezzlement, thereby knocking your judgment into question when you inevitably stood up for him. I pretended to go along with it, but in reality I've been gathering my own evidence. I don't have a whole lot, but I was planning to record our next conversation."

"It's lucky, then, I've been recording this one," Sterling said, holding his phone aloft.

Everyone turned to Peter who began to bluster. "You're going to trust them over family?"

"I don't even know exactly how we're cousins. If you'd be so kind as to clean out your office, I'll have security escort you out," Alby said, an impressive amount of steel in her tone.

"You can't fire me," Peter hissed. "Your dad brought me on. He wanted me to take over."

"He wanted you to help me take over, but you've been trying to subvert me for years, and I'm tired of it. I don't play games, Peter, and I don't reward disloyalty. My trust in you has been irrevocably broken. I wish you well in your next endeavor, but you can't stay here. We're done."

He blinked at her, furious, two spots of color in his cheeks. Sterling was glad he and Hart were there for this discussion because, judging by the amount of anger in Peter's eyes, he wasn't certain Alby would be safe otherwise. "You're an idiotic child who is more interested in making eyes at her boyfriend than running this company. I'll be the first to throw a party when you run it into the ground."

"I think that's about enough," Hart said, saving Sterling the trouble. "If you want to preserve yourself the dignity of being physically tossed from this office, I'd suggest you leave now."

Peter stalked out, bumping Hart's chest hard on his way. After he was gone, the three remaining people stood in a silent little triangle. "I better make a note to take him off my Christmas card list," Alby remarked quietly, and Hart and Sterling chuckled. The tension was broken and she took a step toward Sterling. "Still, this is a nice surprise."

"I didn't get a chance to set everything up," he said, presenting her with the flowers he'd been attempting to water. "Daffodils and two lips."

She smiled. "My favorite. They look a bit dry, I'm going to give them a drink." She took them from him and stepped into the bathroom, leaving Hart and Sterling alone.

"Thank you for that," Sterling said. He had sensed the temptation warring in Hart, and he was glad propriety won.

"I don't fight dirty, Sterling," Hart declared, his posh Atlanta accent a stark departure from Sterling's low country one. "But I do fight." He tapped his hand on the door and made his departure.

Alby returned from the bathroom a minute later. "Did Hart leave?"

"Yes."

She smiled. "I think he's going to be a wonderful addition to the company. Everybody likes him, and he knows his stuff."

"Excellent," Sterling replied, hoping he didn't sound as stiff and forced as he felt. Hart Wentworth was everything he wasn't—wealthy and cultured chief among his virtues. Alby set the flowers on her desk and sank tiredly into her chair. Sterling picked her up, took her seat, and settled her in his lap. "You look tired."

"I'm all done in," she admitted, resting her head on his shoulder. "Plus the thing with Peter, ugh."

"You did great," he said, rubbing a little circle at the base of her spine. He felt the tension drain out of her.

"I don't enjoy that sort of thing," she admitted.

He chuckled. "Albertine, I know. You're sweet as sugar. But sometimes it's necessary to play the heavy, and you were perfect. In charge without overplaying it. You deserve this company and absolutely no one could run it as well as you do."

She pressed her face to his neck. "Thank you." Her lips moved against his skin, and his heart started to thud. His hand eased up and down her spine.

"You hungry?"

"A bit," she said, sliding her arms around him.

"What are you doing tonight?"

She eased back to peer up at him. "What'd you have in mind?"

"How about I'll cook for you and we'll watch a movie," he suggested, suddenly desperate to spend time with her, just the two of them.

She tipped her head, pretending to consider. "Which movie?"

He blurted the first movie that came to mind, which turned out to be a mistake. "*Ernest Saves Christmas.*"

She laughed. "Classy, but it's not Christmas."

"Isn't it? It's felt like it every day lately," he said, his hand smoothing over her bare calf.

"Boy, you make me swoon," she said, leaning up to press her lips to his.

Girl, same, he thought but couldn't say it because he was too busy kissing her senseless and being kissed senseless in return.

CHAPTER 25

Sterling made burgers while Alby sat on the high stool in her kitchen and kept him company. She wanted to know everything that had been going on the last few days while they were apart, and he filled her in as he worked.

"Why you lookin' so serious now?" he asked, noting her pensive expression.

"Because you've been knocking yourself taking care of everyone in your life, and now you're here taking care of me."

"Yes, but I like taking care of you and, unlike with those others, I intend to seek a reward when this night is through." He wagged his brows at her and was rewarded when she smiled and blushed. It did things to him, that blush. Made him feel protective in more ways than he normally might have been. Other women he'd been with demanded so much from him, expected everything. Alby asked for nothing, gave everything, and was as pristine and innocent as fresh snow. The combination made him want to physically shield her from anything that might harm her or beguile her.

"You shouldn't have to cook for me. I have a housekeeper for that," she noted.

"Woman, you bother me. I *like* to cook for you." He had the sudden vision of himself, years down the road, in this very kitchen, cooking supper each night while he waited for Alby to come home from the office. He didn't hate that vision, didn't hate it at all. If he wanted to be with her, he would have to accept a softer role than the one he'd always imagined. Alby would be the breadwinner. He would likely be the primary caregiver and overseer of the house. Their roles would be reversed. Could he handle that?

"I lost you," Alby said softly, touching her fingers gently to his hand.

He jerked to attention and tossed her a smile. "Nah, you've still got me."

She giggled, and his smile widened. "You just can't help yourself from being charming and saying these adorable things. It's like you've been in training for it our whole lives."

"Everything up to now has been practice," he said, winking.

"Oh, boy," she muttered, and he laughed.

"If it's any consolation, you have an overload of charm yourself, Albertine."

"That is not true. I have never successfully flirted with anyone in my life."

"That's debatable, but I'm not talking about flirting. I'm talking about that smile, and those eyes, and all that mass dose of sweetness. You about knock me off my feet."

"Silly," she said, not believing him at all.

"Alby, Alby, Alby. I'm going to have to convince you." He gave her a patented Sterling look then, the kind that made her toes curl.

How many girls, she wondered and cut herself off. It didn't matter if none of it was real to begin with.

"Now I lost you," Sterling said.

She gave herself a little shake, pasting on a smile. "No, it's been a long week. But this looks and smells amazing."

"I must admit to a bit of pride in my burger technique, although I've never used one of these fancy indoor grills before. I hope that doesn't mess with the outcome."

"I'm certain they'll be delicious, Sterling. Know why?"

He grinned. "Cause you think I'm good at everything?"

"I know it. You've been biologically programmed to excel in all the best possible ways."

"Knowing what high standards you set, I'm going to take that as the compliment it is," he said sincerely. Alby was good in all the ways. If she thought he was, too, there must be a bit of truth to it. He found the more he got to know her, the more her opinion meant to him.

He plated their food and sat to eat.

"I knew it would be good, but this exceeds my expectations," she said, pausing to dab grease and cheese from her lips. "How would you like a job as my personal chef?"

"Depends on the perks," he said, tossing her a look that made her cheeks flush.

"Goodness," she murmured, and he chuckled.

"I'm not ready to give up on my store quite yet, though," he said, frowning thoughtfully as he stared unseeing at his burger. Instead he saw his store. He'd hired a retired librarian to look after it while he worked at Alby's company but the additional cost meant he barely broke even. How was he ever supposed to get ahead?

"I've been thinking about that," Alby said.

"What have you been thinking?" he asked, reaching over to snatch the uneaten third of her burger. It was a win-win, her inability to eat more than a birdlike portion and his raging appetite.

"You're a good project manager, Sterling. Really good. I've heard so many complimentary things about you, your work ethic, your enthusiasm, your people skills."

He squinted at her, swallowing the last bite of burger. "Why do I feel like I'm about to be fired?"

She smacked his hand with her napkin. "Of course you're not, crazy boy. The point I'm making is that you are a really good project manager. I could not be happier with your performance. But in all the time you've worked at my company and in all the meetings we've had together, I have never once heard you use the enthusiasm you used the day you showed me your store."

He blinked at her, trying to parse her meaning. "Okay. Thank you? I'm not certain I get where you're headed."

"The store is where your heart is. You should be pursuing that."

Before he could open his mouth to tell her he had no idea how to make it work, she continued.

"I thought of a couple of things that might help," she said meekly, staring at her water glass, unaware of the way he stiffened.

"Oh?"

She forced her eyes to his. "The thing is, I own your building."

He blinked again, faster this time. "You…what?"

"When Hayden's dad had his first stroke a few years ago, I bought the building so he would be able to keep his repair shop in place while he recovered. He never recovered, but then Hayden came along and opened the shop and… The point is that I own the building. It's ridiculous for you to keep paying me rent when I neither want nor need it."

He made no comment, remained staring at her in mute surprise. Unsure of what his silence meant, she pressed on.

"There's more. I serve on a charity board in Atlanta with Martelle Dixon."

When he didn't respond, she hastened to explain.

"She owns *Fox Chase Bookstore*."

"Wow," Sterling exclaimed, despite himself. *Fox Chase Bookstore* was a destination bookshop in Atlanta, one of the premiere bookstores in the country, an Atlanta institution and destination all in one. "I hope I get to meet her sometime."

"Well, I'm glad to hear you say that because I texted her about your store. She's highly intrigued and wants to come visit."

"She wants to visit my store?" he said.

Alby nodded. "Yes, she's very community minded, always looking to give people a boost. You'll like her a lot, I'm certain, and she'll likely have a lot of suggestions about how to improve your bottom line."

He cleared his throat and set his napkin on the table. "You think my business is in need of help."

"Isn't that why you're working for me?" she asked gently.

He'd always believed his business had a hard time making it because he lived in a small town without much traffic. But Alby made it sound as if it was his fault he didn't succeed, as if he didn't know what he was doing. It stung more than he might have imagined. He retrieved his napkin, warping it between his fingers.

"You look mad," she whispered. "Did I overstep?"

"Mad?" he said, his voice matching hers in volume, if not tone. "Why would I be mad? Because my billionaire girlfriend thinks I'm a business failure? Why should that trouble me?"

"That's not… You said you didn't have a problem with my money, you said you deferred to me in matters of business, you said we were for pretend, but you keep calling me your girlfriend."

Sterling wadded his napkin and tossed it into a tight ball on the table. "Looks like I didn't mean any of it," he snapped. Alby flinched, stricken, but he was too angry to notice, too angry to do anything but storm from the house and drive away.

CHAPTER 26

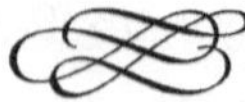

Duncan Shepherd got it at last, the reason everyone talked about thirty as if it were some magical line of demarcation between childhood and becoming an adult. Four months from his thirtieth birthday, and all he wanted to do was sleep. Or maybe it wasn't turning thirty. Maybe it was because he now spent half his week with a newborn who preferred to be walked well into the wee hours of the morning. Whatever the reason, childhood was over and sleep was his new soul mate. Any time he wasn't working, he was sleeping, as long as it was Chelsea's turn with the baby. It was the only way he could survive his turn with the baby.

So it wasn't unusual that he was sleeping at eleven on a Friday when his phone buzzed insistently. Groggy and half asleep, he picked it up and said hello, flipping it when he spoke into the wrong end.

"Duncan, it's Alby."

He sat up and swiped a hand over his face. Albertine Mowry hadn't called him since they were fifteen and working on a joint project for social studies. "Hey, girl, what's up?"

"I don't suppose Sterling happens to be with you," she said, and it was her tone more than her words that alarmed him.

"No. What's wrong?"

180

"We had a bit of a disagreement. He was upset and, well, I'm a bit worried about him."

Duncan was instantly worried, too. He had no idea how much Alby knew about Sterling's recent struggle with depression. Did she know he had contemplated suicide? Had nearly jumped off a ledge? That, in fact, Duncan had been the one to pull him down? Or was this merely Alby being Alby and worrying about everyone in her world?

"I'll find him," he promised, reaching for his pants and keys. "Do you want me to have him call you when I do?"

"I don't think he will. Just tell him…tell him I'm sorry and…just that, I suppose. Tell him I'm sorry."

"I'm sure whatever it is will blow over, Alby. You know he doesn't stay mad long," Duncan said. He didn't add what he was thinking, that he had never seen Sterling the way he was with her, smitten, over the moon, practically drowning in laser beams of love.

"I think this time might stick, and maybe it's for the best. Anyway, I just want to make sure he's okay. Thank you, Duncan."

"You're welcome," he replied, but he was frowning as he hung up. What on earth happened between them? Last time Duncan spoke to Sterling two days ago, he was talking about forever with her. He hadn't been surprised by the sudden announcement as much as he was surprised not to be surprised. Somehow they fit. It was more of a wonder they hadn't happened before now.

He drove to Sterling's house and let himself in. His mother glanced at him with a smile, some girly British show on TV. "Oh, hi, sweetie. Sterling's not here. He's with Alby."

"I know, but he said I could borrow his tennis racket," Duncan lied with ease, tossing her a smile as he walked down the hall to Sterling's room. He let himself in, turned on the light, and looked for any clues to his whereabouts. There were none. He checked his phone to see if Sterling had replied to his text. He hadn't. Flicking off the light, he strode back down the hall, pausing outside Birdie's room. He turned on her light and looked around, inhaling her too familiar scent. *Birdie. My girl.* No, not his girl, Hayden Paxton's girl. He flicked off Birdie's light and strode down the hall, anxious to leave the house now.

"Goodnight, Mrs. T.," he said, smiling once again at Sterling's mother, his second mom.

"Goodnight, sweetheart," she returned absently, not turning her attention from the television before her.

He closed himself in his car and thought. *Where would Sterling go if he was upset about Alby?* And suddenly he knew. The answer was obvious.

He drove downtown and let himself in Sterling's store. It was dark but unlocked. "Sterling," he called in case he was sitting there in the dark. It would be beyond creepy to stumble over his inert form in the unlighted shop, like a horror movie. There was no answer and no sound within, but the back door was cracked, a light in the hallway. Where did that door lead? *To the roof.*

Suddenly Duncan was sprinting through the store and up three flights of stairs. He burst onto the roof and saw Sterling standing at the edge, peering out. "Don't do it," he shouted.

Sterling spun to him, hand on his chest. "Oh, man, you nearly gave me a heart attack."

"Better than splattering on the sidewalk," Duncan declared, reaching his side in record time. He bent over, clutching a stitch. When had sprinting turned into such an ordeal?

"You think I was about to jump?" Sterling asked, sounding shocked.

"Precedent," Duncan said, sucking oxygen.

"I'm upset, not suicidal. Believe me, I know the difference by now." He turned and slid down the wall, bringing his knees to his chest. Duncan sat beside him.

"Your girlfriend called me," he said.

"You mean my fake girlfriend?" Sterling asked, tone bitter.

"What?"

"Alby thinks we've been faking it all this time," he said.

"I thought you told her it was fake," Duncan pointed out.

"I did, but obviously things changed."

"Did you tell her that?" Duncan asked.

"No, but we've been inseparable, we've made out, I slept in her bed. How could she not know?"

"Sterling, it's *Alby*," Duncan said. "She's always been the most innocent, oblivious girl of our acquaintance. How many men has she dated?"

"None," Sterling said slowly, the light beginning to dawn.

"How many women have you dated?"

"I sort of lost count," he said, tone grudging.

"So you told her she was your fake girlfriend and expected her to read your mind when you changed it mid-stream? She must be some kind of psycho if she couldn't keep up with your mental whims."

Sterling sighed. "Fine, I'll give you that one, but there's other stuff."

"What other stuff? I'm batting a thousand tonight." He mimed striking a ball with a bat and shaded his eyes, presumably to try and see his homerun.

"She doesn't want me to pay her rent on my store," he threw out, tone belligerent.

Duncan blinked at him. "She owns this building?"

"Yes, she does."

"So your megarich girlfriend, who doesn't need your money, doesn't want you to pay her rent, and you have a problem with that?"

"I don't like the feeling it gives me," Sterling said.

"What feeling, success? Come on, man, I've seen your books. Rent is your biggest expense. Without it, you could actually afford to live on what you make. And you're complaining why?"

"Would you be okay with a woman giving you things?"

Duncan stared at him, openmouthed. "It's like you don't know me at all. If I could find an Alby, I'd be content to never work again. Pay me for services rendered, baby. I'll be your beck and call boy." When Sterling shot him a look of disgust, he bumped his shoulder. "Reverse the situation. Would you charge her rent?"

"I… No. That would feel weird. But she's so…She's so much more than what I am."

"Yes, she is. Let's hope she never realizes," Duncan said. When Sterling remained quiet, he sighed. "Come on, man. You and Alby, you're two peas in a ridiculously good pod. You're both so upstanding I feel the need to double down on being a horrible person, just to balance you. You've been so happy the last few weeks since you reconnected. Don't lose that. Don't make my mistakes. Believe me, it's not worth it."

"She suggested I meet with someone to help me with the bookstore."

"Who?"

"A woman who owns a really successful bookstore in Atlanta."

Duncan sat up, frowning. "Wait a minute, are you trying to tell me your girlfriend wants to arrange a meeting with someone successful in your field who might mentor you toward finding that same sort of success? I hope you denounced her as a witch."

"Yeah, but…I…and she…" He stared into space a few beats before covering his face with his hands. "I messed up so bad. Why do I keep doing that with her? I mean it's Alby. Why does it seem impossible to not make a complete fool of myself in her presence?"

"You tell me," Duncan said.

"Because I…because…*Oh*, wow. Now what?"

Duncan smiled. "Now you go and get your girl."

Sterling sprang up but regarded him uncertainly. "What if she won't see me? She blocked me before. She's good at it."

"Then you work around it. Come on, man. You're Sterling Thompson. Do you really need more of a pep talk than that?"

Sterling grinned at him. "No." He disappeared, sprinting as fast as Duncan had arrived. He remained on the roof, enjoying the view, the stillness, the serenity.

"A thousand and one," he remarked, miming another homerun.

CHAPTER 27

Alby took a sleeping pill. She hadn't taken one since her parents died. Back then sleep had been an impossibility. It had seemed so again tonight after Sterling stormed out. How had everything gotten so messed up? Had she actually done something wrong? That was the part she kept coming back to. Was it so wrong to not charge Sterling rent? To set him up with the owner of the most successful bookstore in Atlanta? *I don't think it is.* Why, then, had it made him so angry?

The sad fact was she didn't know enough about men. In fact she knew nothing. When Hart texted her to ask some innocuous question, she almost laid out her problems for him. But even she, in her limited experience, understood it was wrong to talk about her problems with one man to another one.

So she took a pill and went to bed. Maybe everything would look better in the morning. It usually did.

The pill worked its magic and she sank into a deep and dreamless slumber for a few hours until someone repeatedly shook her shoulder. Unable to rouse herself completely, she did the only thing that came to mind. She flung out her hand and smacked him.

"OW!"

Whose voice was that? And in her bedroom, no less. She should wake up, see who it was and why he was there. But she was so tired…

"Albertine."

Her eyes flew open at the use of her full name. Since her parents died, only one person used it.

"What is wrong with you?" Sterling asked, his face impossibly close to hers as he squinted into her eyes.

"Did you wake me up to yell at me some more?" she asked, dazed.

"Are you drunk?"

"Of courshe not," she slurred, curling back into a sleepy ball. Like a startled caterpillar. Caterpillars were cute. Was she giggling? Yes.

"Alby," Sterling said, and now he was shaking her shoulders, bouncing her up and down on the bed.

"Whee," she said.

"Baby, what is wrong with you?"

Her eyes flew open, finding a semblance of sobriety with the endearment. "Why you here?" What was wrong with her lips? Were they swollen? She poked them. No, not swollen, merely unusable. Her tongue poked out, smoothing over them. Sterling's eyes fastened on her tongue, following its progress.

"I need to talk to you."

"Did you break in?" she asked.

"Yes. I watched you enter your code when we arrived home the other night."

"Cat burglar." Her finger poked his chest. "Meow."

He leaned forward, smelling her breath, likely checking for hints of booze.

"Sweepy pill," she informed him. "Sleep. Sleeping." Her tongue smoothed over her lips a few times. They seemed to be there, but weren't fully functioning.

"Maybe you should lie down," Sterling suggested. He gripped her biceps and gently pushed her back. "I wonder if you'll remember any of this in the morning. Maybe that will make it easier."

"Make woot easier?" she asked.

"First, my heartfelt apology. Call it groveling, if you want. Alby, I'm so sorry. Again. It might surprise you to know I don't usually have to apologize this much in relationships. I acted like a complete…I can't think of an adjective bad enough for my idiocy. You were being your usual kind and helpful self, and I threw that in your face." His hand skimmed her forehead, pushing back her hair. She blinked at him, owlish. "Second, I need you to know this was never fake for me. Ever. I lied through my teeth because I wanted to be with you so badly, and I was scared of how much I wanted to be with you. So I pretended it was all fake as cover."

One of her eyes slid closed while the other remained fully open, wobbling precariously as it stared at him.

"The thing is, I'm in love with you. So completely and ridiculously in love with you, you have no idea. I want to get married and have babies and I don't care that you're a bajillionaire. I'll sign a prenup. I'll sign ten of them. I don't want the money, all I want is you. You're like some kind of precious gift from heaven that's fallen into my life. And of course you were right and I should meet with Martelle. Part of being a good businessman is realizing you're in over your head and in need of help. I know she can help me turn my store around, and I'm willing to listen."

She was still staring at him with one eye, but she was also snoring. Laughing, Sterling bent forward to kiss her softly. She didn't respond. He stood, shucked out of his clothes until only his boxers remained, and slipped in beside her.

* * *

IN THE MORNING, Alby woke feeling that horrible post-pill groggy feeling. It was why she stopped taking them in the first place, because waking felt like an out-of-body experience. And she'd had such strange, vivid dreams. Starring Sterling, of course. Thoughts of him sent a stabbing pain through her heart. She missed him, missed him so much she could practically smell him. She sniffed and froze. *Could* she smell him? Was that some weird after effect of the pill?

She tried to sit up but was instead weighted down by someone's arm across her waist. She lifted the blanket and looked at the arm and then the body it was attached to. Why was Sterling in her bed?

"Morning, baby girl," he whispered, pulling her tight against him and nuzzling her neck.

"Um," she said, heart thudding.

"You don't remember," he said.

"What, uh," her voice cracked. She cleared it and tried again. "What don't I remember?" She pulled the sheet up again. Was she dressed? Yes.

"Mrs. Thompson, how could you forget?"

She bolted upright. "What? We got married?"

He grinned up at her. "Don't I wish, but no. We did make up, though. It was epic."

"How epic?" she squeaked.

He wagged his brows at her. She peered beneath the covers again. Laughing, he tugged her close and bundled her against him. "Let me recap for the sleep impaired. I apologized, you forgave me. Not in so many words, but I got the gist. I declared my undying love. I'm still waiting to see how that one turns out."

"You…what?"

He reached up and pressed his palm to her cheek. "I love you, Albertine. And because I'm starting to know the way your mind works, let me assure you I have never once said those words to another woman, never come close to feeling them. I love you in all the ways, for all time."

"You broke into my house in the middle of the night to tell me you love me?"

"Is that not how it's done? There's a learning curve for these things. Next time I'll know."

"You, Sterling, love me, Alby." She touched her finger to his chest and then hers.

He nodded.

She blinked at him a few times, dazed, and then her face slid into a satisfied smile. "I cannot tell you how glad it makes me to hear that." She lay down, resting her palm on his belly button

"Yeah? Do tell." He skimmed his palm on her back, smiling when she gave a little shiver.

"See, I'm incredibly relieved because I volunteered us to watch Bess and Hogue's kids this weekend while I send them away to a resort to sort out their problems, and I had no idea how I was going to do it alone."

"Huh," he said, dimple disappearing.

"But also there's the little fact that I adore you."

"Yeah?" he said, dimple popping.

"I warned you in the beginning I would only fall once and fall hard, and yet you relentlessly pursued me. You have only yourself to blame for my devotion now. If you thought I was a clinger when we were kids, you underestimate the tenacity age has bestowed on me. There's no getting rid of me now, Sterling. You can try, but you will not succeed."

"Hallelujah, because I come with an immense amount of baggage, beginning with mental illness and ending with parents who believe I'm their personal valet."

"Bring it, 'cause when you get in trouble, I'll cling harder. It's my nature as a barnacle."

"We should probably never work in advertising. To the outside observer, we don't sell ourselves well."

"We'll keep it between us, then, and put on a perfect front for the outside world," she declared.

"I love it," he agreed. "Let's make sure to post pictures of our perfect, amazing life together all over social media so no one will ever guess how hard we're struggling or how near to broken we are."

"I'm already thinking of which filters to use to tone down the crazy," she said, holding up her hand for a high five. He smacked her palm and kept her hand, bringing it to his lips for a kiss.

"I love you. I don't ever, ever, ever want to do life without you again, because I'm fully aware of the before and after. You're my safety net, my soft place to fall. Plus you're adorable and a good kisser. Truly, I've hit some kind of lottery I didn't realize I entered."

"There are so many good things I could say about you, Sterling, but they all fade away every time I see you in your boxers in my bed."

"Are you trying to tell me you only want me for my body?" he asked.

"Pretty much yes," she agreed, smiling.

"I can live with that," he said. "What happens when I'm old and the body fades?"

She smoothed her hand over his abs. "I plan to make a lot of memories to sustain me."

"I feel like you're getting the raw end of the deal here because I want you for your heart and mind, things that will be with us forever. And you only want me for something that has a decade left, at most."

"I think you underestimate exactly how good you look in these shorts," she said, snapping his waistband.

"Baby, I really don't," he said. Smiling, he tipped her face and kissed her.

THANK you for reading *Saint Sterling,* the second book in the Georgia Peaches trilogy. For more books, please check out my website at www.vanessagraybartal.com.

ACKNOWLEDGMENTS

Special thanks to macro vector and pch.vector for cover art.